Steven sat with his fingertips together, tapping his lip. "So you had a great job out there, huh?" His eyes narrowed.

Jeanie's throat tightened. What did he know? "Y–yes."

He nodded, then stood. "You really don't want to talk about this, do you?"

"It was a hard time. I thought I'd made the best decision for you. You have to believe that."

"Yeah. You said that." He walked toward the door. "One last question and I'll try to leave it alone. Was there someone else? Did you meet someone before your birthday? Is that the real reason you didn't come home?"

The answer screamed in her brain. *Yes. But not like you think. Not a boyfriend. I met someone. And I couldn't get away.* "No. There wasn't anyone else."

He nodded. "You know, there is one more question." Blue eyes scanned her face. "When did you stop loving me, Jeanie?"

"I nev—" She gasped. That wasn't what she'd meant to say.

He smiled. Gentle. Sweet. He walked over to her. The backs of his fingers brushed her face. "That's all I need to know."

And he walked out, closing the office door behind him.

A Wisconsin resident, **BECKY MELBY** has four sons and nine grandchildren. When not writing or spending time with family, Becky enjoys motorcycle rides with her husband and reading. Becky has coauthored several books with her writing partner Cathy Wienke for Barbour Publishing.

Wisconsin native **CATHY WIENKE** and her husband have two sons, a daughter, and two grandchildren. Her favorite pastimes include reading and walking her dog. Cathy has coauthored numerous books with her writing partner Becky Melby for Barbour Publishing.

Visit their Web site at www.melby-wienke.com.

Books by Becky Melby and Cathy Wienke

HEARTSONG PRESENTS
HP98—Beauty for Ashes
HP169—Garment of Praise
HP242—Far Above Rubies
HP822—Walk with Me
HP837—Dream Chasers
HP857—Stillwater Promise
HP874—Pleasant Surprises

Don't miss out on any of our super romances. Write to us at the following address for information on our newest releases and club information.

Heartsong Presents Readers' Service
PO Box 721
Uhrichsville, OH 44683

Or visit www.heartsongpresents.com

Parting Secrets

Becky Melby and Cathy Wienke

Heartsong Presents

In loving memory of my mom,
Dorothy Archer Schwenn,
for what was, what is, and what I longed for. . .
"I can only imagine. . ."
Cathy

To our newest blessings:
Keira Soleil, Oliver Liam, Lillyanne Alice Lola,
and Caden Luke Melby
Love you with all my heart, Grandma Becky

A note from the Author:
We love to hear from our readers! You may correspond with us by writing:

**Becky Melby and Cathy Wienke
Author Relations
PO Box 721
Uhrichsville, OH 44683**

ISBN 978-1-60260-779-8

PARTING SECRETS

Our mission is to publish and distribute inspirational products offering exceptional value and biblical encouragement to the masses.

PRINTED IN THE U.S.A.

one

Jeanie Cholewinski leaned against the reception hall door and waved one last time at the Ford Explorer covered in white paper bells. Evading the blue eyes of the man beside her, she bent down and forced trembling fingers to detach a satin bow from the collar of her daughter's Irish setter. She pressed her cheek to a copper-colored ear. "They'll be back in two months, Sunny."

When the silence grew heavy, she stood, raised her chin, and faced the man who'd haunted her dreams for thirty years.

Running a hand across his graying beard, Steven Vandenburg cleared his throat. "I imagined a million reasons why you disappeared." His gruff tenor cut the summer air as he nodded toward the fading taillights. "*She* wasn't one of them."

Jeanie stared at his profile, not trusting her instincts to gauge his tone. Too many years had passed since she'd prided herself on reading Mr. Vandenburg like a book. "I know."

Broad shoulders rose and fell in a jagged sigh. "You owe me some answers. Can we go get some coffee?" His gaze fixed on the spot where the headlights had vanished.

Jeanie repositioned a hairpin, willing her fingers to cooperate. Coffee with Steven sounded both tantalizing and terrifying. If he didn't ask too many questions, if he didn't push too hard for answers, coffee with Steven would be more than she'd let herself hope for.

The door behind them squeaked on its hinges. Jeanie turned and smiled at the maid of honor. "Hi, Pug."

In shorts and bare feet, Patti Pugelli dangled white sandals from her fingertips. Slinging a lavender gown in a filmy bag over one shoulder, she put her arms around Jeanie and sighed. "Happily ever after."

Jeanie nodded. "Keep praying for them."

"I will." Pug's hold tightened. "Wade's a prince. He'll treat Angel like gold." She lowered her arms. "I have to get on the road."

"Did you take leftovers?"

"My backseat is as stuffed with pastry as I am. I've got *kluskies* and *kolacz* to last all week. And that was absolutely the most beautiful and scrumptious wedding cake I've ever tasted."

"Thank you." Jeanie kissed her daughter's roommate on the cheek. "Drive careful, honey."

"I will."

Pug walked down the steps, and Jeanie turned back to Steven. Her eyes gravitated again to wide shoulders and traveled down to muscled arms. Uninvited, an image of those arms surrounding her took up residence. She blinked and took a deep breath for courage. "I want to change first. Would you like to come over to the house?"

"I don't want to upset your mother."

"How old are you now, Steven?" she teased, trying to lighten the moment. "Fifty-two and you're still scared of my mother?"

A hint of the smile she once knew tipped his mouth. "How about the Log Cabin?"

Jeanie bit the corner of her bottom lip as memories turned like faded pages of a yearbook. Coded messages across a crowded room. . .letting their eyes speak for them because they couldn't be seen together in public. "They've totally remodeled it since. . .recently."

"Is that a yes?"

She nodded. It had to be a yes. No matter how tired she was after the craziness of her only daughter's wedding, she owed him the next hour.

No, she owed him the past twenty-nine years. . .with Angel. With *his* only daughter.

"I'll go put my jeans on and—"

Screeching tires, rubber scraping the curb, and the slam of a car door ended her sentence.

"Jeanie! Jeanie!" Her mother slid from behind the steering wheel and jumped out of the car. Flowing leopard print cascading over purple slippers, she charged toward them, short legs taking the steps two at a time.

"What happened? What's wrong?" A fire at the bakery, a break-in at home. . .dozens of scenarios flooded Jeanie's imagination before Ruby Cholewinski caught her breath enough to explain.

A legal-sized envelope materialized from the folds of her dress. "Open it."

Jeanie grabbed the envelope. A stylized French chef in the upper left corner cranked the tempo on her pulse. "Grégoire Pâtisserie!" The envelope fluttered in her hands like a moth anxious for escape. When she finally got it open, she read the words silently, tears springing to already tender eyes. "I'm in! I'm going to New York!"

Her mother squealed. As Jeanie wiped her eyes she caught Steven's confusion and handed him the letter. "It's a national pastry competition. I've been chosen to compete at Grégoire Pâtisserie in New York City. First prize is a year of study in Paris."

"That's wonderful. Exciting. Congratulations." Steven's expression conflicted with his words.

His lack of excitement disappointed her. He had, after all, been the one to paint the first broad brushstrokes of this thirty-year-old dream. She answered with a sad smile. She couldn't expect him to rejoice with her. He was still staggering from the news she'd given him yesterday. How long would it take him to embrace the knowledge that he had a daughter? "I'll go change clothes."

"What for?" Her mother's piercing gray gaze dashed from her to Steven and back again.

"We're going to get coffee. Will you take Sunny home?"

"*Hmph*." Her mother turned on her soft purple heels, patted her thigh for the dog to follow, and stomped back to the car.

Jeanie grabbed the door handle. "I'll be right back." *And then I'll give you answers. But only some of them.*

﹡

The woman who sat in front of him was a stranger.

Steven hugged his coffee mug as Jeanie, across the table from him, chatted with the bald, black-suited maître d'. . . in English smattered with Greek. Where had she learned Greek? All these years of wondering about her and feeling guilty for wondering, and maybe the person he'd once thought he couldn't breathe without no longer existed. The girl he knew—the girl he shouldn't have known the way he did—possessed the heart of a poet and the curiosity of a child. This confident woman prattling on about a French chef whose name sounded like "Gray Gwah" reflected so little of that innocence. She'd had only one ambition back then. . .to love him.

He studied her profile, noticed the fine lines that branched from the outside corners of her eyes and deepened when she smiled. Her face was thinner than the last time he'd touched it, and time, like a skilled sculptor, had added angles and curves to the rest of her. He'd once told her she was the cutest girl in school. At forty-six, the word that fit her was stunning.

One thing hadn't changed. Deep brown eyes transported him to a time of furtive glances and moonlight trysts—a time best left in the shadows of the past. Regret, a familiar companion, made its presence known in the tightening in his chest. *If only. . .*

The maître d' held out a manicured hand. "I know you just ate wedding cake, but I must bring you *saganaki* on the house. Okay?"

Steven's stomach roiled at the thought of the deep-fried

cheese he'd loved with a passion so many years ago, but he shook the man's hand and thanked him. "We wouldn't dream of turning that down."

Jeanie thanked the man and turned coffee-colored eyes back on him. "You knew before I told you, didn't you? That Angel was yours?"

Pressing his finger onto the tines of his fork, Steven felt the sharp edges of the question that had taunted him for nine months, since he first met the girl with blue eyes like his sons' and his mother's red hair. "I did the math. But there was no way I could be sure she was mine."

Jeanie flinched. His insinuation had to hurt. Her eyes closed for a moment, then followed a waiter with sizzling plates. She turned back. "I understand."

Her head tipped slightly to the right, making a silent groan rise from his belly. He remembered that look. *I can read you like the Sunday comics, Mr. Vandenburg.* Could she still?

Her arms crossed. "I thought if you'd put two and two together you'd call."

"It wasn't my place. I have a little pride, Jeanie. I wasn't about to pick up the phone and ask if I'd fathered your daughter." He rocked the fork, letting the handle bang the wood planks on the table. "When I saw you in Chicago last fall and you ran. . ." The ache of loss came back with a rush. He'd gotten only a glimpse of her across the reflecting pool at Millennium Park. A glimpse, and then she'd turned and run. "I knew you didn't want anything to do with me, and I didn't want to do anything to hurt Angel."

"Steven." Her fingertips grazed his sleeve. "I'm sorry." Her eyes searched his for a long, wordless moment. "How *are* you, Steven?" Her question flickered the flame in the amber glass holder between them.

How are you? Did she really want him to answer that? Did she really not know that her decision to stay in California without a single word had scarred every inch of his psyche?

That her selfishness had insured a life that always felt second-best? He swallowed every angry retort and finally managed "God is good." In truth, in spite of his shattered hopes, it summed up his life to date.

"He is."

"And how are *you*?" The way the words left his tongue showed he hadn't really forgiven her the way he'd once convinced himself he had.

"I'm good. Hitting my stride a bit late in life, but I finally know what I want to do when I grow up."

"And what is that?"

"I want to teach. At a pastry school."

"Wow." Why did her announcement put his chest in a vice?

"I started taking classes in St. Louis when Angel was in grade school, but my father died and I gave it up. I tried a few more times, but something always came up—car repairs, Angel's tuition—and I'd have to go back to the bakery full time. It's taken me awhile to recapture my dream, but a chance at this contest is another step toward my goal."

"Where would you have to go to teach?"

Her eyes sparkled. "Realistically, Chicago."

He took a gulp of ice water.

"But my dream goal is Paris."

An ice cube lodged in his throat. He coughed and gasped.

Her hand rested on his arm. "Are you okay?"

"I'm f–fine," he rasped. His breathing finally calmed, and he gave her an embarrassed smile. He wasn't ready to lay his feelings on the table, but choking on her words probably accomplished just that.

She pulled her hand away. "Angel says you have two sons."

He nodded. "Griffin is twenty-five. He's still single and working in Tacoma. Toby's nineteen. He's going to school in Boston. They're good guys."

"I'm so sorry about your wife. How long ago did you lose her?"

"It's been almost four years. We had a good life together." Well-worn guilt surfaced. They had built a good life. But he'd given Lindy second-best.

The casual catch-up talk suddenly irked him. They weren't old school buddies touching base after thirty years. He wasn't ready to share the details of his life. And he couldn't feign interest in what she was doing now until he understood what she'd done then. "Did you know you were pregnant when you left?"

She drew back as if his hand, instead of his words, had slapped her. She looked down, tucking a stray strand of hair into the lacquered braids and purple jewels that crowned her head. Did she still hate hair spray? Why, in the midst of his anger, did he suddenly want nothing more than to yank out the hairpins and watch her hair fall to her shoulders?

"I found out I was pregnant two weeks after I got to Aunt Freda's. I should have realized it sooner, but I di—"

"Why didn't you call me?" *Did you really love me? Is Angel really mine?*

Her eyes shimmered as she raised her head. "It would have been the end of your career, Steven."

"So?" His fist hit the table. "Jeanie. . ." His voice strangled on her name. "You knew that wouldn't have mattered. I would have flipped burgers or cleaned toilets to be with you. I thought we had honesty. I thought. . .you knew me." A sigh ripped from his throat.

"Steven, I was seventeen. You were my teacher." She leaned forward, her gaze latched onto his. "You would have been charged with statutory rape."

❧

Jeanie watched as the truth found its target. The muscles on his jaw slackened. His lips parted, but he didn't say a word.

"I would never have let that happen to you." Her voice sounded odd to her ears—soft and hushed. She wrapped her hands around her coffee mug to steady them.

Slowly, he nodded, giving her time to study the way the years had altered him. He'd changed, but not in the ways she'd expected. His dark blond hair had thinned and whitened at the temples. She guessed he'd added a good fifty pounds, but he carried it well. The weight made him seem strong, protective, though his expression at the moment was just the opposite.

Those eyes. . .hurt, transparent. . .and the same shade as Angel's. Her daughter's eyes had been a constant reminder of Steven. His voice hadn't changed either, and that unnerved her. "Staying away from you was the hardest thing I ever did," she whispered. He'd never know what that decision had cost her.

"You should have told me."

"I didn't tell you because I *did* know you. You would have done the noble thing. And you would have been fired and humiliated and probably gone to jail." Her hand loosened its grip on her mug and she reached out to him, touching his sleeve. "Your family would have disowned you."

His hand clamped over hers with an intensity that scared her. "Jeanie—"

A waiter rounded a corner with a red tray. A waitress approached and poured brandy over the square of cheese on the tray. A click, a tiny light, and suddenly the dish erupted in orange flames that shot three feet in the air. "Opaaa!" The waiters yelled and doused the flames in lemon. "Cheers!" Gingerly, she slid the black plate of browned cheese onto the table.

"Thank you." Jeanie smiled apologetically at Steven. "Life goes on, doesn't it?"

"Never the way you plan."

"Never."

Steven ran a hand over his beard. "It's going to take me awhile to sort this out. Eventually, we need to move past this, but I can't until I'm sure you understand something."

With her hand still covered by his, all she could do was nod.

"I would have gone to jail, Jeanie. I would have given up my career and faced whatever humiliation the school district or my family would have thrown at me. If you'd come back on your birthday the way we planned, we could have figured it out together. Do you understand?" Blue eyes stabbed her. "I would have done anything for you. . .if you'd given me the chance."

Turning away from the honesty in his eyes, Jeanie blinked back tears.

But not if you'd known what I did to survive.

two

Hairpins mounded on the bathroom counter as stiff curls sprang free. Jeanie yawned and dropped two more pins. With her free hand, she turned a page in a cloth-covered book and read the ending of a poem she'd just written.

> *I returned the gift he gave,*
> *Though she wasn't his to keep,*
> *And as he gave his child away,*
> *God brought us back together.*

Closing her eyes along with the book, she wiped a stray tear. *Lord, I am in awe of You. In Your time, You have answered my prayers. Whatever happens from here on is also in Your hands.*

She stared out the window of her apartment above her mother's garage. Lights turned out on the porch next door, leaving the miniature lilacs blooming between the houses bathed in moonlight. It was a peaceful scene. She scooped hairpins into a plastic bag and turned on the shower. She didn't want the smell of hair spray invading her sleep. And tonight she would sleep.

Maybe better than she had in thirty years.

The wedding was over. She was going to New York. And finally, Steven knew the truth. The only secrets she harbored now were the ones she never needed to share.

Steven knew. Tonight, she would sleep.

❧

Why, after what she'd done, had he protected her? Protected her from the emotions that brought him out on the deck at two in the morning.

14

Steven sat on the edge of his hammock, but the sway of his usual sanctuary nauseated him. He stood and walked down the deck steps. Motion sensor lights flicked on. He bent and picked up a cold and damp steel horseshoe. The stakes were lost in darkness, but that didn't matter. He drew his arm back and let it fly. It hit the fence with a *thud*. He picked up three more and let them fly. *Thud. Thud. Ding.* A little self-restraint on the last one earned him a ringer. He congratulated himself with a fist in the air. A momentary victory over bitterness.

She should have told him. Whatever she claimed as her reasons, it boiled down to one thing. Selfishness. She'd done what was best for herself. Not what was right. . .for him, or for Angel.

He could easily picture Angel as a little girl, red curls bouncing, chubby little legs running. To him. That little girl needed a daddy. And he'd needed a daughter.

How many times had he and Lindy picked out girls' names? How many pink paint swatches had his wife collected over the years? But after two uncomplicated pregnancies and births, she'd suffered three miscarriages in a row. The first sign that something wasn't right.

Even if Jeanie had told him about Angel years after he was married, he would have been there for his daughter. Lindy would have been there for his daughter. She would have accepted his past and accepted the consequences with him. That's just the kind of woman she was.

At some point, he was going to have to confront Jeanie with the truth of his feelings. For now, he just needed sleep.

His eyes swept the darkness, envisioning his backyard in Texas. A tree house, a fort. . .yet there would have been room for a pink and white playhouse.

It wasn't likely he'd sleep tonight.

ъ

Jeanie rubbed tired eyes. The Monday after your only daughter marries should be an official day of rest.

As she turned on the bakery's OPEN sign at six thirty, the phone rang.

"Angel Wings Bakery. This is Jeanie."

"Jeanie, I can't come in this morning." The voice of their only full-time employee shook.

"Sue? What's wrong?"

"We had to take Bradley into the ER. He's been up all night with stomach pains. Hey, I gotta run. I'm so sorry. Can you cover till your mom comes in?"

"Of course. I'll be praying. Call me when you know something."

She set the phone in its cradle as the door opened and more than a dozen silver-haired tourists in matching blue jackets swarmed the bakery.

"Morning everyone. Welcome to Angel Wings, where Polish pastry touches the heart." She handed a Morning Glory muffin to the first woman in line and counted out change. Tour busses paid the bills.

She emptied two pots of coffee and made two more. The chairs filled and customers stood outside. Three men took the only stools at the counter. A man in a faded yellow shirt and red bow tie pointed to his name tag. "Name's Joe Crow, sweetheart. Can't forget a moniker like that now, can you?"

Furrowed cheeks puffed on the man beside Joe. "Ah, don't pay him no never—"

A coffee cup clunked on the front counter. Jeanie reached out and took it. "Can I h—" Her breath caught as she stared at the man's garish parrot tattoo. *Just like the one. . .* Her pulse hammered. The cup crashed to the floor.

Just a flashback. Refocus. Relax. She turned away, then back to the man who held out his cup for a refill. *Just an illusion.*

"Well, well. All the way from Reno. . .and after all these years. . . Small world, isn't it? You haven't changed a bit." Apelike fingers reached out and ran along her arm.

Jeanie stumbled back, knocking the phone off its hook.

Her arms crossed her chest; her fingers bit into her shoulders.

"What a nice surprise." The man was far too old for his bluish-black hair. A black moustache, so thin it could have been penciled, curved in a sneer. "I've been sitting over there staring, and I finally figured out why you look so familiar." An evil laugh rumbled across the counter. "You're a long way from home, Misty."

"I'm not. . .who you think I am." Her back pushed against the phone. *There's nowhere to run.*

He laughed and reached into the pocket of his short-sleeved black shirt. Red letters below the pocket spelled out *DIAMOND JO CASINO, DUBUQUE*.

Jeanie's heart squeezed as though the man held it in his thick hands. *Oh, God, why is he here?*

The man pulled out a pair of glasses and squinted at her name tag. "Jeanie, huh? Doesn't suit you. Call yourself whatever you want—it doesn't change who you are."

"Denny?" A blond, maybe in her late thirties—the one who'd ordered two cups of coffee and a single *chruscik*—laid a hand on the man's arm. "Let's go."

"Anything you say." He took off his glasses. Black eyes smoldered. "We'll be back. Gotta have some more of that pastry." His gaze crept from the top of Jeanie's head to her name tag. "*Misty.*" He turned on his heel.

The blond took two steps toward the door, then turned and eyed Jeanie with blatant suspicion. "Do you know her?"

Another evil laugh. "Not nearly as well as I'd like to."

Jeanie dropped to her knees, the pieces of the broken cup blurring before her eyes.

"Are you all right? Miss?"

A shard stabbed her finger. Blood dripped as prickles skittered across her arms. Voices blurred. She was back in that room, Angel in her arms. And just outside was the man with the parrot on his arm, talking to her through the door, making promises she prayed he'd never keep. In the distance, she heard the men at the counter asking if she was all right. She stared at the bottom shelf below the cash register. *We could hide there. We'd both fit. Don't cry, baby. Angel, please don't cry.*

"Miss? Did you get cut?"

Refocus. Breathe. Be somewhere else. She blinked, nodded, and looked up. "I'm fine. Just fine."

೪

Summer break used to be the best part about working for the school system. Until Lindy died.

When he was teaching, he'd had two and a half months free and it had never seemed long enough. Now that he was a principal, his contract gave him only two weeks. . .and it seemed to last forever.

Turning up his iPod, Steven rode his year-old John Deere mower out of the shed. He'd bought it at the same time as the house when he'd moved up here from Dallas.

As he cut the first swath, he tried to focus on the week ahead and not the Saturday behind him. Mondays, the first of five long days he'd have to fill with something, were hard enough. Thoughts of unsaid words to Jeanie would only make them seem longer.

He'd only made one sweep around the backyard when his phone vibrated in his shirt pocket. He put the mower in neutral and checked his caller ID. Jim Hansen, calling from his daughter's place in Maryland. Thank God for Monday morning friends. He turned off the mower. "Hey, Jim."

"Steven. You won't believe this. I met someone." Jim's staccato voice beat faster than usual.

"Someone. . .like a woman, you mean?"

"Of course a woman. Cindy set me up. Didn't want any part of it. But she's amazing."

Steven laughed. "Jim, you can't leave the Sorry Widowers! We have a pact."

"Ha. Just wanted to beat you to it."

" 'Ha' to you, too. So what's she like?"

"Her name's Amanda. She's pretty and nice. And she can cook. Kind of like your Texas woman."

Steven pushed his Cubs cap back on his forehead. "I don't have a woman."

"Yeah. Okay. So what've I missed?"

Leaning against the backrest, Steven sifted through the weekend events he was in the mood to share. "Another exciting weekend. Burt and I mowed Mrs. Simpson's lawn on Saturday and went to see Oren Willmar in the nursing home. Burt took Emma to Fried Green Tomatoes after church and I had dinner at the Larsen's."

"Wow. Lucky you. Turkey lasagna?"

"Of course."

A high, raspy laugh came through the phone. "So sorry I wasn't there. Anyway, gotta run. Going to brunch with Amanda. Just wanted you guys to pray. Need to be wise about this. Any requests?"

If he gave even the condensed version of the news he'd had confirmed on Friday, the lawn would never get mowed and Jim would miss his date. "Pray for wisdom for me, too. Got a lot going on. I'll explain when you have time."

"Will do. See ya."

Steven tucked his phone back in his pocket and prayed for Jim as he started the mower again. The smell of freshly cut grass and the song filtering into his ears elevated his Monday frame of mind. *Let me fight through the nothingness of this life.* Matthew West sang "The Motions," and the lyrics pumped conviction into his veins. Though at times, especially at the beginning of a long, lonely week, it felt as though his heart had stopped when Lindy's did, he knew he still had purpose. *Lord, let passion for You consume my thoughts and my days.*

As he cranked the wheel to the left, his pocket vibrated once again. He stopped the mower and pulled out his phone.

Gretchen. Interesting timing, considering Jim's comments. "Hello?"

"Steven. I'm in Houston this morning. I've only got a minute between meetings. Guess what?" Her breathless question sent nervous tingles down his arms.

"What?" *Lord, I'm confused enough right now. . .*

"I just heard they want me to do photo shoots in Iowa this week. I'll be in Dubuque on Thursday." Her voice rose like a child opening a birthday present. "And I'm taking Friday off."

"Wonderful." It was. Really. "Should I book you a room?"

"There are no other options, are there?" Her soft tease fed his confusion.

He didn't bite on the bait she'd dangled. "I'll call and see if the Sunshine Room is open. What time will you be here?"

"I'll come over and make you breakfast on Friday morning. How's that sound?"

A bit too cozy. His palm felt damp against the phone. "See you then."

"Can't wait. Love you."

He tried to swallow but couldn't. He looked longingly at the glass of iced tea sitting on the deck railing. "You, too. Bye."

❧

"Go home. I'll stay." Jeanie pointed Sue toward the back door. "You have a sick boy. That's all you need to be thinking about."

"You took over for me yesterday. I can't do this to you two days in a row." Sue's weary eyes welled with tears. "You've been here since four."

"And you've been here since five. Get. I have nothing else to do today and I hardly ever get to work the front. Go."

"I just hate to do this to you, and I'm afraid it's going to happen a lot." A tear slid down her pale face. "Now that we know it's Crohn's disease. . ."

"I've been thinking about hiring someone part-time for summer anyway. Now that the wedding's over I can concentrate on that. But that's my problem. Go home and take care of Bradley. And sleep."

Sue walked out. The side door closed and silence pressed

against Jeanie's ears. She didn't usually mind being alone. But the nightmares spawned by the man in black infused her consciousness as though he still leered at her over the counter. As though he still had power over her. She locked the door. "Whatever is true, whatever is noble, whatever is right, whatever is pure, whatever is lovely, whatever is admirable—if anything is excellent or praiseworthy—think about such things." The verse from Philippians slowed her heart rate.

The buzzer on the front door sounded and she jumped. "Be still, and know that I am God," she whispered. She tried to check her reflection in the window of the deck oven, but the yellowed glass made her look jaundiced. If she won the contest in New York, the ancient appliance would disappear. And so would she for a while.

But, by then, would she still want to? She smoothed back a few wayward tendrils and tried to do the same with the question. With a deep breath, she left thoughts of Steven in the kitchen and walked to the front of the store. "Morning, Lucas." She smiled, the remnants of her nightmares evaporating in the presence of the friend she'd known all her life.

"Mornin', sweet pea."

"How's business?" Jeanie poured a cup of coffee for the man who owned the jewelry store across the street. Though he'd been born in Galena, Lucas Zemken's accent was as thick as his Welsh-born father's. Finger tracks showed in silver-streaked hair. More lines marked the corner of his right eye than the left—earned by forty years of squinting into a jeweler's loupe.

"Ah. . .love is in the air." He pointed at a cherry-filled *kolaczki* in the display case.

"Lucas, you're a unique breed. You're in love with love, but too chicken to try it yourself." Jeanie handed him a medium coffee with two spoons of sugar. She pulled a piece of bakery tissue from a blue dispenser box and put two pastries on a paper plate.

Lowering his glasses, he looked at her over the top rim. "One could maybe say the same of you, sweet pea."

"Sooo. . ." Jeanie scrunched her nose at him and side-stepped the jab. "Selling lots of engagement rings?"

"Not lots. I *wish*. But enough to pay the bills." He sat on a stool, then swiveled to face the front window. They'd had very few face-to-face conversations since Lucas was always facing his store, watching over the tops of parked cars for his door to open.

Lucas raised his cup in a toast. "To the best wedding cake baker this side of France."

"Oh, Lucas, I know you say that to all the girls."

"It was a beautiful wedding."

"Wade's ring is amazing."

Smile lines crinkled on Lucas's right eye. "It is, isn't it? And do you know what is engraved inside?"

"No. Should you be telling me this? Isn't there a jeweler-client privacy act or something?"

"Nah." His fingers formed an imaginary loupe. "It said. . .are you ready for this? It said 'She loves you, yeah, yeah, yeah.'" He took a swig of coffee then appeared ready to spray it all over the bakery.

"Seriously? All that fit on a ring?"

Lucas patted his chest. "Takes a real craftsman. And as long as we're speaking of 'She loves you,' I've been waiting to get the scoop. I nearly fell off my chair when I saw this strange man walking Angel down the aisle."

Jeanie sighed. "You and everyone else."

"Makes me wonder what other secrets you're hiding. He's a nice guy."

"He is."

"And. . .?"

"And. . .God alone knows the future. I'm glad it's out in the open and Angel can get to know him."

"Where was he all these years?" One fist lodged at his hip.

"Put your shotgun away, Mr. Dillon. It wasn't his fault he wasn't around. Let's just say I was in a bad place and I couldn't see any point in bringing Steven in with me."

Lucas pressed his lips in a firm, hard line. "So what now? He's single, you're single."

"We'll see. We're not the same people we were back then."

"What was your visceral response the first time you saw him after all these years?"

"Visceral response? Any other guy would say 'gut reaction,' but you—"

"Just answer the question."

Jeanie lined up boxes of herbal tea as the answer brought her back to the moment. Last October, at the Crowne Fountain in Chicago, she'd looked across the reflecting pool and there he was. "Visceral response" didn't come close. "Lightning bolt" would almost describe it. Heart slamming her ribs, painful sting in her eyes, the whisper in her head—*Steven. . .it's you.* It was as close to an out-of-body experience as she was likely to encounter. Her imagination ran to him, dropped her to her knees in front of him. And then rational thought swept in and she ran. Away from him.

She threw an empty tea box at the wastebasket. Short of breath, as though she'd just turned her back on Steven and fled into the trees, she took two quick inhales. "No violins or fireworks. I was just scared about his reaction—"

Lucas slid off the stool. "I'm sorry. I've got a customer." He pushed his breakfast to her side of the counter and patted her hand. "I'll be bock"—his Arnold Schwarzenegger impression fell flat—"because I'm not really buying the nonchalance, sweet pea." He took several steps but stopped when a man walked in front of the window and reached for the door handle. "Ho ho. Look who's here." Lucas turned and winked. "Definitely not buying the nonchalance." He laughed, greeted the man, and waved.

And Steven walked in.

three

He glanced away from the fat little baker on the wall with a clock for a stomach, but Steven was sure the hands started spinning backward at the speed of light. He was twenty-two again, days away from beginning his first year of student teaching. Alone and not in the mood to fix his own breakfast, he'd wandered into town. It was a growling stomach that first introduced him to the girl who now stood, older and more beautiful than ever, behind the pastry case.

Jeanie smiled as he took a stool at the counter.

"Coffee and *chruscik* please."

Another customer walked in. As Jeanie filled a bag with long johns and bismarcks, Steven poured in the cream and sugar she'd set in front of him. He hadn't used cream and sugar in twenty years. Taking a bite of the "angel wing" he closed his eyes. The smell alone reversed the hands of the clock. The first time he'd met Angel, at a picnic with Wade, the man who was now her husband, she'd brought *chruscik*. It was his first clue, though it hadn't registered until she'd left. Red hair like his mother's, and a sweet taste that could only come from one bakery. . . .

"Steven?" Jeanie stared at him, her smile now wary, from the other side of the counter. The other customer was gone. Had the door buzzer sounded when he left?

He hadn't even said hello. It seemed too late now. "I was wondering if we could get together to talk sometime."

"I. . .we could talk now. The morning rush is over. My mother will be here in a few minutes to work the counter." She nodded toward the back. "Let's go in my office."

He followed her into a tiny green-walled room. It couldn't

24

have measured more than eight feet square. A desk, two chairs, and shelves on all three walls were piled with books and papers—neat, clean, but cluttered. He took the chair across from hers.

She cleared a spot for his coffee. Her braid swung over her shoulder. She'd worn her hair loose when they first met, but braided it every day in the weeks before she'd left for California. Had she really worn the same style ever since? No woman he'd ever known did that.

Jeanie sat in a scuffed leather chair. "Not very often you're on that side of a desk, I imagine."

His thoughts flew back to the first time Jeanie Cholewinski sat on the other side of a desk from him. The first of many private, literary magazine meetings. In the first thirty seconds he'd slaughtered her name. "*Janka Chow-link-ski?*" She'd tossed long brown hair and jutted her chin. "*Janka is Polish for the feminine version John. I prefer Jeanie—that's French. And it's Cu-leh-win-ski.*"

He smiled. "Feels kind of strange." Something about the swing of that braid took the muscle out of his emotions. "Jeanie. . ." He leaned forward, set his elbows on the arms of the chair, then changed his mind and crossed his arms over his chest. He had no idea where to start. The Mr. Vandenburg who normally sat on the other side of the desk and had the power to make smack-talking teenage boys quiver in their Nikes suddenly felt like a freshman caught smoking in the restroom.

Jeanie leaned against the back of her chair. Her eyes dimmed.

"This is all history for you, Jeanie. For me, it's like opening an old wound. I know we can't change anything." He ran his fingertips up and down the middle of his forehead. "I just need to understand. I've thought through what you said about me going to jail. That would have been bad, but it wouldn't have been forever. It wasn't an insurmountable problem. The girl I thought I knew would have called, would have wanted to work it out together." He leaned forward. "Make me understand, Jeanie."

&

Dampness prickled beneath her arms. She hadn't perspired like this since junior high. She had barely enough saliva to moisten her tongue. "I was young and scared and alone." *If you knew how scared and why. . .and how alone. . .* "I maybe wasn't thinking as clearly as I should have been."

"But you had nine months to think. You had twenty-nine years to think. Didn't you once, in all that time, come to the conclusion that I should know?"

"You were married. . . ."

"I got married *three years* after you left." Bright blue eyes drilled into her. "Not even a phone call before that?"

"You moved to Texas."

"You could have found me. The school had my parents' address. I made sure your friends knew I was going to Dallas. I was in the phone book."

Her breathing became shallow. *Refocus. Pray.* But even the words that used to bring moments of clarity triggered shuttered, hidden images. She needed to pull away. *Into the corner where it's dark and he can't see. Angel, don't cry. Please don't cry, baby.* The buzzer announced a customer and dispelled the memory. "I'll be right back."

A woman with two small boys stood at the counter. Fingerprints multiplied on the display case as the boys pointed out sprinkle-covered doughnuts and frosted cookies. The mother apologized for their indecision. "Take your time." *Please.* A thud and the jingle of keys sounded in the kitchen. Her mother was here. And the office door was wide open.

The children finally made up their minds. Jeanie bagged two cookies and threw a third in for free for a frazzled mom who looked like she was counting her pennies. "Enjoy."

"Thank you. You didn't have to do that." She waved as she walked out. "This is the brightest spot in my day so far."

A hand touched Jeanie's back. "What's *he* doing here?" Her mother's voice seemed more worried than harsh.

"He just stopped in to talk. There's still a lot he needs to know."

"There's still a lot *I* need to know. About him and his intentions."

"I know. We'll talk." Something her mother had seemed unwilling to do since Friday. She gave her mother a quick hug and walked back to the office.

Steven sat with his fingertips together, tapping his lip. "So you had a great job out there, huh?" His eyes narrowed.

Her throat tightened. What did he know? "Y–yes."

He nodded, then stood. "You really don't want to talk about this, do you?"

"It was a hard time. I thought I'd made the best decision for you. You have to believe that."

"Yeah. You said that." He walked toward the door. "One last question and I'll try to leave it alone. Was there someone else? Did you meet someone before your birthday? Is that the real reason you didn't come home?"

The answer screamed in her brain. *Yes. But not like you think. Not a boyfriend. I met someone. And I couldn't get away.* "No. There wasn't anyone else."

He nodded. "You know, there is one more question." Blue eyes scanned her face. "When did you stop loving me, Jeanie?"

"I nev—" She gasped. That wasn't what she'd meant to say.

He smiled. Gentle. Sweet. He walked over to her. The backs of his fingers brushed her face. "That's all I need to know."

And he walked out, closing the office door behind him.

&

Jeanie's mother glared at him as he walked out of the office. He sent a sheepish smile her way and crossed the hardwood floor between her and the front door in as few steps as possible. Outside, the air had warmed considerably. The shade from the awning felt good. He looked up the sidewalk at the redbrick buildings lining the cobblestone street. He loved this town, though he'd avoided it this past year. His address might say Elizabeth, but Galena felt like home.

And now that he felt free to come to Galena, he couldn't very well be at war with one of its residents. *If it is possible, as far as it depends on you, live at peace with everyone.* He turned the corner onto Perry Street, arguing with the butterflies break-dancing in his belly. After three steps he stopped, turned around, and walked back into the bakery.

The office door was ajar. Jeanie wasn't in sight. *Good.* He waited for her mother to count out change into a young boy's hand then stepped to the counter. Her name was Ruby, right? It didn't matter, first names were too familiar. He needed the element of respect. "Mrs. Cholewinski, could I talk to you for a minute?"

"Hmm." Gray eyes sparked. "You may not like what you hear if you do."

He fought a smile, shoved it down again when it pushed to the surface. "I can't imagine what you must think of me."

"No, you can't."

"I can't defend myself, but I'd like to explain. I want you to know I wasn't a. . ." Wasn't a what? A letch? A child molester? "I wasn't a predator."

Ruby Cholewinski ripped a paper towel in half and began cleaning around the knobs on the cappuccino machine. "What were you, Mr. Vandenburg? An upstanding role model for the children in your care?"

Children? "Jeanie was only five years younger than I was. I was a *student* teacher."

"I don't think the law would have made that distinction. You were a legal adult. She wasn't."

"I loved your daughter. More than I could ever put into words. I was the advisor for a school magazine. We spent a lot of time working together. We had a relationship. It was wrong, I know. I spent hours. . .weeks. . .on my knees over that. But you have to understand that I wasn't taking advantage of her. We were in love. I wanted to spend the rest of my life with Jeanie. She doesn't know it, but I had a ring." *Still have a ring.* "I was going to propose to her on her birthday. I know we were young, but. . ." The faraway look on the woman's face made him stop.

She set the paper towel on the counter and faced him, bracing her hands on the counter. For a long, uncomfortable moment, she simply stared. He felt as though he was undergoing a wordless interrogation. Did she, like her daughter once did, have the ability to read his thoughts? If so, she'd find nothing deceptive in what he'd claimed.

Finally, she nodded, ever so slowly. A faint smile smoothed her lips.

"I believe you, Mr. Vandenburg."

☙

Jeanie dropped onto the only clear spot on the couch. It was after nine on Wednesday night, and she'd been up since four. The pillow-top mattress in the next room called to her, but two plastic bins on either side of her called louder.

She yawned. Nightmares had turned to night terrors that stalked her waking hours. The energy it took to push them back was taking a toll. She'd had years to work on forgiveness, more sleepless nights than she could ever count to wrestle with God and barrage Him with "Why?" and God had not failed her. Peace had been her companion for many years. Until one Sunday in September—an uneventful brunch with Angel and her new friend, Wade Ramsey. She'd been minding her own business, humming a praise song while she washed dishes, when Wade dropped a name that stole her peace. *Steven Vandenburg*—the new principal of the school where he taught.

She didn't believe in coincidence. God had brought Steven back into her life for a reason. But that reason might not include rekindling their relationship. *"That's all I need to know,"* Steven had said yesterday. She could still feel the warmth of his hand brushing her face. He'd read the truth in her eyes. . . . Would it end up hurting him?

God was in control. That conviction had brought her through much worse. But if her theology was accurate, it meant He'd not only brought Steven, he'd also brought the man in the black shirt. The man who'd stood guard outside her room for three years, who was once again imprisoning her with vestiges of a fear she thought she'd left behind forever.

God knew all things, but all she was sure of at the moment was confusion. Running both hands over her face, she sighed.

The box to her right overflowed with cookbooks and cake decorating magazines. The one on her left held fifteen years worth of mementos—Angel's life, all but the first three years, in photographs, crayon drawings, and school papers. She pulled out a faded report card and smiled at a comment on the back. *Angel is very polite and kind. I would like to see her participate in class more.*

In Tuesday's restless predawn hours, she'd decided to make a scrapbook for Steven. Tangible evidence of all he'd missed would be painful, but maybe glimpses of Angel's past would fill in some blanks and keep him from asking more questions.

Kicking off her shoes, she scooted back on the couch. A battered purple notebook, the spiral binding kinked and stretched, slid off the pile of Angel's keepsakes. "My Diary" scrolled across the cover in silver glitter. Jeanie opened it and stared at the date on the first page. Angel's thirteenth birthday.

> *Dear Diary,*
>   *I know I'm too old for pretending, but birthdays are different. I think every year on my birthday, even when I'm an old, old lady, I will always pretend that the doorbell rings and there is my father. He says "Surprise!" and then he*

hugs me and tells me why he had to stay away. Sometimes he is a spy for the CIA and sometimes he is a movie star. But always, when he hugs me, it doesn't matter anymore that he missed all my other birthdays.

The clack of Sunny's nails on the outside step announced a visitor. A knock followed.

"Come on in."

Her mother walked in and set a covered dish on the small kitchen table. "What's wrong?"

Closing the notebook, Jeanie looked up. "Nothing."

"You're crying."

A single tear dropped off her chin and onto the silver glitter. "I'm fine." She took a deep breath, willing unruly emotions back between the pages of the notebook.

"Mm-hmm." Her mother walked across the kitchen, pushed aside a stack of travel magazines, and sat on the trunk that served as a coffee table. Her very presence spoke volumes. "The tuna casserole is a peace offering."

"Thank you."

"It was silly, but I reacted the same way I would have if I'd found out the truth at the time you got pregnant. All I could think about was that man taking advantage of my little girl and wonder how I could have been so blind."

"You weren't blind." Jeanie rubbed a kink at the base of her neck. "I was deceitful. I worked very hard at making sure no one knew. And Steven didn't take advantage of me. I knew what I was doing."

Her mother nodded. "I know. And I'm ready to leave it all in the past. God and I had a little talk and I think I'm done wanting to take you over my knee."

"Thank you. And Steven?"

A ghost of a smile tipped her mother's lips. "I think he's suffered enough for his sins."

"He'd be happy to hear that."

"He already has."

"You talked to him? When?"

"I have my ways. Maybe it's time I started keeping a few secrets from *you*." The quick smile she'd kept hidden for days loosened a few of Jeanie's tight muscles. "So where does he fit in? Is he part of the family now? Do we invite him for Christmas? Sunday dinner?"

Jeanie laughed. "If Angel wants to include him, I'm fine with it."

"Angel, huh?" Her tone was anything but subtle. "It's pure serendipity that man is back in your life. A Godcidental discovery. Not a coincidence." Her eyes narrowed. "You still care about him."

"Of course I care. He gave me Angel. But we're totally different people now." There was no sense in stirring her mother's probably dormant hopes that her daughter would someday marry. There was nothing she could do about her own hopes. She slid Angel's bin onto the floor. "They say you have a complete cell turnover every seven years. That means I've been four whole new people since high school."

With a shake of her head, her mother stood. "With that logic, I've been three whole new people since I became a widow. Every one of those three new people was in love with your father." She walked toward the door, then turned around and smiled. "I'm not so sure all your cells are out of love, *Janka*."

four

Steven picked up the kitchen phone and set it down again. He'd lost track of how many times now. He dumped the burnt-edged crust from his pizza into the trash under the sink and glanced at the clock. It was nine fifteen in Boston, three hours earlier in Tacoma, Washington.

His boys were probably busy on a Thursday night. Toby would be scarfing pizza—most likely as burnt as his—with his study group. He could easily picture Griff schmoozing a client over dinner.

But just when was a good time to tell your grown sons they had a sister? He didn't quite know how to word it. *Hey, Griff, you sitting down? Tobe, you'll never believe this. . . .*

Maybe he'd wait until his own astonishment had worn off a bit. He brushed crumbs off the pizza pan and was sticking it back in the cupboard when the doorbell rang. After a quick scan of the kitchen—not too messy—he opened the back door. "Burt! Come on in."

"Put your shoes on. We have a mission." Burt's communication skills were a product of his years in the Navy.

"Yes, sir."

Steven dug his shoes out from under his recliner, grabbed the drugstore bag that contained what he'd bought for Jim and Burt just this afternoon, and joined Burt on the back step. At sixty-three, Burt still ran three miles a day and lifted weights. Rock-hard arms, resting on his knees, boasted tattoos that told stories of what he referred to as his "brain-fried years."

Burt nodded toward his 1971 Warbonnet Yellow Corvette convertible. "Emma's sump pump quit working. Supposed to rain before midnight."

Staring at the sleek slope of the front of the car, already imagining the wind in his thinning hair, Steven finished tying his shoes and stood up. "I love doing ministry with you."

"We'll get extra jewels in our crown for these sacrifices. Ready?"

Steven followed Burt to the car and leaped, far less gracefully than Burt, over the door and into the seat. As he fastened his seat belt, he looked up into a cloudless sky. "Emma's pulling your leg."

"Yeah, I know."

"Bet she busted her own sump pump."

"Probably."

"When are you going to propose?"

Burt laughed and put the car in second, spitting gravel all the way to the end of Steven's drive. "I'll shave my head in mourning when you take the plunge, but I won't be following you. When you going to put a ring on Gretchen's finger?"

"Look! A fox." Steven pointed toward a white-tipped tail disappearing into the woods.

Burt laughed. "That's not the fox you're supposed to be talking about." He turned onto the highway and had the machine doing sixty in seconds.

Steven ran his hand along the sleek gold finish on the outside of the door. Corvette Therapy. It worked every time. The rush of wind in his ears, the hum of tires on pavement, melted Steven's tension. "Burt, I need to talk to you about something."

Easing on the brake, Burt nodded. "Spill it."

"There's something I haven't told you about my past."

"Hey, we all got bones in our closets." Burt pulled to a stop sign and turned to face him. "What is it?"

Pressing his lips together, Steven reached in his pocket and pulled out something pink. He handed Burt a bubble gum cigar.

"It's a girl."

❧

Emma Winter eased down her basement steps with two glasses of lemonade. Setting the tray on the floor beside Burt, she turned to Steven. "Tongues are wagging about you, Steven."

"About me?"

"Didn't you see how people stared on Sunday?"

"He's a man, Em." Burt picked up a glass with a greasy hand. "We don't have that sixth sense thing you women got going on."

Emma pushed pale silver bangs to the side and sighed. "No more accurate statement was ever spoken. So is it true?"

Steven handed a wrench to Burt. "That I'm oblivious to gossip? Pretty much."

"Is it true you have a daughter that you didn't know about until she asked you to be in her wedding?"

Steven wasn't generally a blusher, but the warmth creeping up the back of his neck probably glowed in the dim basement light. "That's pretty close to the truth."

Emma turned over an old galvanized metal bucket and sat on it. "Her mother owns Angel Wings in Galena, right?"

"Yes." Steven cringed inwardly as Burt set down his glass and crossed one arm over his chest. The knuckles of his other hand supported his chin and his eyes widened with the rapt expression of a child settling in for a bedtime story. Steven took a long, slow draught of lemonade. "Angel Cholewinski is my daughter."

"I know her grandmother. Used to be friends of sorts. I remember when Ruby's daughter went to California. I thought something was fishy. So it was all because you—"

"Let's just say I made some unwise decisions when I was young and leave it at that."

Emma's hand oscillated in time with her head. "Your past is just that. We've all got skeletons, and I know God's dealt with your closet like He's dealt with mine."

Steven cocked an eyebrow at Burt.

"It's your present that counts. Was the news really a shock?"

With a quick glance at Burt's knowing smile, Steven nodded. In spite of what she'd just said, by the time the new sump pump was installed, Emma would have wrangled a book's worth of details about the past she claimed didn't interest her. "I first met Angel back in September. Her new husband taught at my school. In my gut, I knew she was mine the first time I heard her last name. She has my mother's hair color and the same eyes as my boys. But denial is a handy thing. Hearing it put into words when her mother confirmed it was still a shock."

Wrapping a navy cardigan tighter over her middle, Emma leaned forward. "I'm sure it was. So you've stayed friends with her mother this whole time?"

Excellent work, Emma. "No. We lost touch before Angel was born. I never knew her mother was pregnant."

"Oh my. . ." Emma's prayer chain wheels were almost visibly turning. *Please pray for Steven Vandenburg as he adjusts to the shocking news that he fathered a child out of wedlock. . . .* "So how does it stand between you and the girl's mother now? Are you angry? Or was it your fault you never knew?"

Burt's hands shot into the air. "Whoa. . .slow down, Emma. Give your victim a breather."

"You're right. Steven, I just want you to know I care. Is there anything the church can do to reach out to your daughter? If they don't go to Ruby's church I could invite them to ours."

Steven patted her on the shoulder. "Thank you for your concern, but they're both solid believers, involved in their churches."

"Well. . .isn't God good? In spite of all the dark spots in your past, He saw fit to draw every one of you to Him. What a testimony. That's what you need to tell people to shut them up, you know. God's plan is perfect in spite of us. You just ignore those busybodies at church. Like I said, your past is your past."

It may be my past, but I'm guessing it's about to be everybody's business.

੩

Travel mug in hand, Jeanie stepped into the halo of lamplight on the sidewalk in front of the house. There was a time she'd hated waking before the birds, but now she relished the quiet. The smell of dew-drenched grass mingled with the scent of the neighbors' hybrid tea roses. For a moment, the only sound was the padding of her work shoes on cement and the faint clanging of wind chimes in the distance. Lights glowed from upstairs windows in the house across the street. Her walk to work was like strolling through a Thomas Kincaid painting. Today, it was her window of peace before the Saturday morning craziness took over.

With one last look at canopies fluttering in the shadows of redbrick buildings, she turned onto Perry Street and took out her keys. Entering through the side entrance, she flipped on the lights and, in a motion that had become automatic, opened the cupboard for a clean apron and hairnet.

As she opened flour bins, cracked eggs, and measured sugar, she imagined the announcer's voice as he handed her the first place trophy. *"And Jeanie Cholewinski is going on to Paris!"*

Lost in thought, she jumped when Sue opened the back door.

"Happy Saturday." Jeanie held up the plastic-sheathed list of orders and her weekend help groaned. "How's Bradley?"

"Back to normal for now." Tying her apron, Sue walked to the sink. As she scrubbed her hands she glanced over her shoulder. "Now that my life is back to somewhat normal, any chance you're going to fill me in on the details?"

"About the contest?"

"No. Congratulations, by the way. That's so cool." Sue

turned around as she dried her hands. "But it kind of takes a backseat to the humongous secret you've kept from everyone."

She'd known Sue for more than twenty years. She'd been Angel's babysitter in her early teens and started working at the bakery in high school. "It was a necessary secret."

Sue sighed. "Your life is like a Hallmark movie."

Jeanie scooped dough out of a bowl, flattened it with her hands on the floured table, and folded it into thirds. Walking over to the sheeter, she plopped the dough down and shook her head. "I've got a good life, but it doesn't qualify for happily ever after."

"Hey, you don't know what the last scene's gonna look like. So. . .what's next? He's a widower, right?"

"Yes, but. . .we're not the same people we were way back then." How many more times would she have to say that?

"You don't really believe that, do you? Was he your first love?"

First. And only. "Yes."

"And you were his?"

"Yes. But he was happily married for a lot of years in between."

"There's nothing like your first love. Something magical about it, something you never really get over."

Jeanie pushed the button on the sheeter and listened to the low-pitched whine as the machine flattened the dough and cut it into perfect strips.

"When will you see him again?"

Bending over her work, she hid a smile. "When I'm done here, actually."

If I don't chicken out.

five

Her pulse thumped in her throat as she maneuvered the winding, tree-lined driveway. Why hadn't she listened to her doubts? Showing up on his doorstep at ten o'clock on a Saturday morning might convey the wrong message. But she'd gotten this far. . . .

She'd found his address in the phone book and debated calling first, but any way she phrased it in her head sounded awkward. If she just showed up, the reason for her visit would be obvious.

What is the reason for my visit? It would make more sense for Angel to give him the scrapbook. Was she being less than honest about her motives? If she could control the scene that waited for her at Steven's house, what would it look like? The picture that came to mind—Steven opening up his arms to her—belonged in the Hallmark movie Sue had brought up, not in her life.

She slowed the car and pulled to the side, then picked up the book. It wasn't anything fancy. She didn't have time for stencils and templates and colored pens, but in spite of its simplicity, she felt good about the finished product. Twenty pages capturing Angel's childhood. . .in Galena.

The thought of actually putting the book in his hands suddenly terrified her. *The mailbox.* She'd write a note and leave the book in the mailbox she'd passed out by the road. The lane opened into a clearing. A large gravel circle would allow plenty of room to turn around. Hopefully Steven wasn't looking out. As she eased to the right, she stared at the house. Mediterranean-style, with massive carved double doors and an asymmetrical roofline. The colors—several shades of

39

brown, windows trimmed in olive green—blended into the trees. On the side, a brick chimney rose above the second story. A fireplace. She'd always wanted a fireplace.

Curiosity suddenly shoved aside anxiety. He'd only lived here a little over a year. What drew him to this place? What did it look like inside? She put the car in park, picked up the scrapbook, and got out. The air was cooler here. She reached back in for a sweater.

A car with an Iowa license plate sat in front of the garage. A rental car. One of Steven's sons, maybe. Did they know about her yet?

Clutching the book like a shield, she walked up to the door and searched for a doorbell. All she found was a heavy medieval-looking iron ring. She knocked it twice against the wood, deciding she'd give him to the count of ten.

"One. . .two. . .three—"

Footsteps. Then laughter. The door opened.

"Jeanie!" Surprise lifted Steven's brows. "Come. . .in."

Two seconds of hesitation—the space between "come" and "in" were all she needed to change her mind. "Actually, I can't stay. I just came to bring you this." She held out the book. "I thought you might like some pictures of Angel."

As he took the scrapbook a strange expression crossed his face. Fear? He seemed to draw back.

"Have a good day, Steven." She started to turn.

Almost imperceptibly, the door opened wider. "Come in. Please."

She wavered, not at all sure she was ready for whatever waited inside—meeting his children or being alone with him. "Just. . .for a minute." She stepped past him. He smelled of soap and something spicy.

Her eyes adjusted to the dim light from a black chandelier with flame-shaped bulbs. They stood in a split foyer. Carpeted stairs led up. Slate-tiled stairs that matched the floor beneath their feet led down. To her right was a bookcase. Amid rows of dusty carved and cast metal animal heads that appeared to come from all over the world, one thing stood out—totally incongruous with its bright colors. . .and googly eyes. "You *kept* it?"

Reaching across her, Steven picked up the mug by one of its handle-ears, dusting it with his sleeve. Bulging, yellow, crossed eyes stared from the aqua-blue face. Purplish, cyanotic lips puckered in a kiss. She'd made it in ceramics class.

"I found it in a box when I moved. Couldn't very well leave it there."

Jeanie touched the lips with the tip of her finger. "It goes so well with your collection."

Setting it back, Steven smiled. "I think so. These are all souvenirs of times I want to remember." His gaze fastened on hers.

Attempting a smile and a swallow, Jeanie wrenched her attention from him and directed it toward a tall, blue-and-white urn at the top of the stairs. "You've traveled a lot." She'd intended to phrase it as a question, but the wording evaporated under his stare. "You have a lot of souvenirs."

He nodded. And his hand slid behind her, just barely touching the back of her sweater. "Come and see the rest of them."

From the third step she could see a grandfather clock and a bust of Shakespeare on a dust-covered stand. From the fifth step she could see the floor-to-ceiling stone fireplace. A huge brass-framed picture hung above it. In front of the fireplace was an Oriental rug.

And a woman.

Wearing a man's flannel shirt.

❧

"Jeanie, I'd like you to meet Gretchen Newman. She's a friend from Texas, up here on business. Gretchen, this is Jeanie Cholewinski."

The woman offered her hand and Jeanie shook it. "Glad to meet you."

"Jeanie. . .and how do you two know each other?"

Gretchen's tone was warm, her smile genuine, but her question had the power to give Jeanie momentary brain freeze. Who was this woman? Jeanie appraised the chin-length, slightly curled hair, professionally done brows and nails. Gretchen had to be about the same age as Steven. She appeared rounded, but not really overweight. At least from what she could tell with the baggy shirt hanging to the knees of her jeans. Steven's baggy shirt, most likely.

How did she fit into Steven's life, and what answer was appropriate? Jeanie smiled back, doing all she could to match the warmth. "We're old friends. We met years ago at the bakery my family owns." It was all true. Nothing else needed to be said.

"You own a bakery? Do you. . .bake?" Gretchen gave a becoming little giggle.

"Six days a week from four to nine a.m."

"Oh my." Gretchen laid a hand on Steven's arm. "She's a sister foodie."

Steven laughed. Nervously. "Jeanie's a sixth generation baker."

Jeanie did a double take. He remembered that? She would have had to stop and think before figuring out if she was fifth or sixth generation.

Gretchen brought her hands together and pressed the sides of her index fingers to her bottom lip. "You're going to help with HIS pizza sale, right?"

"Whose pizza sale?"

Steven shifted from his right foot to his left. "I. . .haven't talked to her about it."

"You're having a pizza sale?"

Gretchen laughed. "It's a fund-raiser. Steven is one of the directors of Hands in Service. They do bake sales to raise money for food pantries and the homeless." Her face brightened with a wider smile. "They're doing a pizza sale on

Fourth of July weekend in Chicago. He works with the kids to make the pizzas. I just assumed, since you're a baker. . ."

"I just"—Steven cleared his throat—"haven't had the opportunity to ask Jeanie if she'd like to help." He turned his blue eyes on her, his expression far too intense for a man asking only for help making pizza. "It would be great if you could come along. I can use as many experienced hands as I can get."

Something about the project resonated in her soul. "I'd love to help." The look of surprise and gratitude Steven shot her upped her pulse to a dangerous level.

Gretchen clapped. "Wonderful. This will be so fun."

"So you're helping, too?" It came out with a slight edge. The last thing she wanted was for this woman to think she was in competition. Even if she was.

"I'll be taking pictures."

"Gretchen is a professional photographer." Steven put his hand on Gretchen's shoulder, then removed it. "She takes pictures for. . .what do you call them? Cookbooks?"

"Sometimes cookbooks. Right now we're doing a series of books on famous American barbeque restaurants."

"Seriously?" A faint current of electricity zipped from the top of Jeanie's head to the bottoms of her feet. A professional food photographer stood two feet in front of her. Her mother would label this serendipity. "So you'll be here for the next two weeks?"

"Oh no. I have to be in Dubuque at four. I'm doing a shoot at Sugar Ray's Barbeque. I'll fly back for the fund-raiser."

"How long will you be around then?"

"Just for the weekend. Why?"

"I'm in the Grégoire Pâtisserie contest and—"

"Say no more. You need amazing photos of your entry."

"A friend of mine's an amateur, but he never gets the lighting quite right." How would Lucas feel about being pushed aside?

Gretchen reached out and laid her hand on Jeanie's arm. "I'll do it. I'll work my schedule around it whenever you need me."

Jeanie blinked twice, then again. "I wouldn't ask you to come back just for that and I'd need to know what you charge before—"

"We'll figure it out. Come—you have to taste the caramel rolls I made this morning." She pointed toward what Jeanie assumed was the direction of the kitchen.

"Good idea." Steven set the scrapbook on a low table.

"What's this? Pictures?" Gretchen picked up the book and opened it.

Jeanie shot a quick look at Steven. His eyes appeared riveted to the book.

"Look at that red hair. . .and curls. What a sweet little girl."

"Thank you." Jeanie offered a tight smile. "She's my daughter."

Steven cleared his throat and took an audible breath. "Actually, she's *our* daughter."

six

Steven gripped the shelf behind Jeanie as if his hold on it could somehow stabilize the teetering emotions around him. "How about those caramel rolls?"

The looks he got in return told him humor was the wrong choice. "Let's go sit in the kitchen. I'll make coffee."

Jeanie was the first to move. "Coffee sounds good." She walked around the corner, leaving him alone with a woman with a polite smile stitched to her face.

"I just found out, Gretchen. I've only known for a week."

She closed the book and looked up at him. The question in her eyes didn't need to be asked. She was leaving this afternoon and he hadn't told her yet.

"It's just all so. . .new." Did he have to be totally honest? Did he have to admit he had decided not to tell her yet? "I haven't even talked to the boys."

To her credit, Gretchen managed a smile. "I don't need to know any more, Steven. I never expected you to tell me every detail of your past."

"Let's go sit down."

She led the way. Jeanie looked up as she stacked two empty juice glasses on top of the two dirty plates in her hand. The sight rocked him. What must she be thinking? He walked over to the sink and dumped the coffeepot. "I made this when Gretchen came this morning, but I'll make a fresh pot." Was that too obvious? Probably, but he was more concerned about Jeanie knowing he hadn't entertained an overnight guest than looking silly.

"I'll warm up the rolls in the oven. The microwave doesn't do them justice." Gretchen opened a drawer and pulled out a

45

box of aluminum foil. It was all too clear she knew her way around his kitchen.

Jeanie wiped off the table. "They look delicious. Where did you get the recipe?"

"It's one my grandmother was famous for. I made a few alterations, but it's essentially hers."

Measuring coffee into a filter, Steven fought a weird urge to laugh. All this nicey-nice chitchat had him strung tighter than a stuck fly reel.

"She used to just sprinkle the sugar on the bottom of the pan and heat it in the oven, but I find if I add a little corn syrup to the brown sugar it makes a much smoother consistency." Gretchen's words picked up speed as she slid the pan into the oven. "I set the oven a little higher, too. Sometimes her rolls weren't quite done. I guess my grandpa liked them doughy, but I—"

"Gretchen. . ." Jeanie motioned toward a kitchen chair and took the one across from it.

Thank you. It might get ugly, but at least the inane chatter and strained politeness would come to an end.

Wiping her hands on her jeans, Gretchen nodded, stared at the chair, then sat down. "Like I just told Steven. . .please don't feel like you have to explain anything. Lindy was my best friend for a long time, but we lived two counties apart." The fingers of one hand patted the table as if she were tapping out Morse code in quadruplicate. "Steven and I. . . we've really just been in each other's lives on a regular basis for a few years so I certainly don't expect—"

Jeanie reached across the table and stopped the table tapping with a hand over Gretchen's. Once again, Steven fought laughter. His first love reassuring his. . .what was Gretchen, anyway? He went back to filling the pot with water. Would they notice if he filled it one meticulous tablespoon at a time? Anything to stay out of the middle of the drama.

"I. . .*we*. . .want you to understand."

We do? Where did Jeanie get the idea she was the spokesperson for both of them?

"I was seventeen when I got pregnant."

"Oh my. So young."

"Young and immature. I wasn't ready to be a mother, but I was even less ready to be a wife. So I never told Steven I was pregnant. It was a selfish thing to do, but, looking back, I know it was for the best."

Really? Says who? And was that really your reason, Jeanie? You weren't ready to spend the rest of your life with me?

"I understand."

I don't.

"But God orchestrated things this past year that were totally out of our hands. My daughter—her name is Angel—fell in love with a man who teaches at Steven's school."

"That wasn't a coincidence." Gretchen's eyes grew watery.

"I know."

Please don't let them both start crying. He stared at the back deck through the window above the sink. In the corner, his hammock beckoned from beneath a limb of a century-old oak. *Beam me up, Scotty.*

"Being a single mother isn't easy. But I think you made a wise decision. Two kids right out of high school would have had a tough time making a go of it."

Water flowed over the top of the glass pot. Steven set it down and shut off the faucet. He walked to the table and put his hands on the back of a chair. "It wasn't exactly like that, Gretchen. The story's a little more complicated than that."

"Steven, like I said, you don't—"

"I was Jeanie's teacher."

"Oh." Gretchen looked down at her empty cup, then back at him. "Oh." She repeated the cup inspection. "You could. . . you could have been charged with. . ."

Jeanie nodded. "That's why I never told anyone."

Gretchen's eyes suddenly flashed wide. "Could you still be charged? Now that people know?"

Steven laughed. Again, he knew immediately it was the wrong choice. "There are statutes of limitations."

"Actually, until about eight years ago it could have been possible." Jeanie folded her hands in her lap. "The laws would have been much harsher if I'd been under seventeen, but still, in some cases they can prosecute up to twenty years after the victim turns eighteen."

Victim? Is that how she saw herself? He pulled out the chair and sank into it.

"Victim is a legal term, Steven. I don't. . .I didn't ever. . . think of myself. . ." Jeanie looked toward the sink. "I'll finish the coffee." She jumped up and went to the sink.

Gretchen shook off her shock like a dog flinging water after a bath. She looked at him and smiled. "Your daughter is so blessed to get to know you."

"I'm the one who's blessed." His eyes suddenly stung. "She's an amazing young woman. It's just beginning to sink in. I have a daughter. . . ."

For all his fears that the women would make a scene, it was just his embarrassing luck to be the first to shed a tear.

❧

As he closed the door after Jeanie, the bug-eyed cup caught his attention. It could have been yesterday he'd torn neon yellow wrapping paper from a lumpy ball of bubble wrap—sitting on a blanket in the center of a grove of aspen saplings behind the fairgrounds, Jeanie's braid bouncing as she laughed at him fighting with an entire roll of tape.

He headed up the steps. As he walked through the living room, he looked over at the leather-bound volume of Shakespeare sonnets sitting next to his recliner. Had Jeanie seen it? Would she be surprised to know an aspen leaf still held their place?

Sonnet 116 was branded in his head, not only from years

of teaching English. Emotion, experts claimed, enhances memory.

> *Love's not Time's fool, though rosy lips and cheeks*
> *Within his bending sickle's compass come:*
> *Love alters not with his brief hours and weeks,*
> *But bears it out even to the edge of doom.*

He walked slowly into the kitchen, picked up the empty cake pan, and ran his finger along the bottom. Brown sugar and butter coated his fingertip. "Jeanie sure loved your rolls." Licking the sticky decadence, he walked over to Gretchen and slid the pan in the suds-filled sink.

She didn't answer. Even before he looked at her, he knew what he'd see. Tears streamed onto the bubbles. His gut knotted and he walked back to the table, pretending he hadn't noticed and hating himself for it. He picked up the sea turtle trivet Lindy had bought in Hawaii and braced himself for the lashing he deserved. "I'm sorry I didn't tell you sooner. I should—"

"No, I don't care about that." She turned around and leaned against the sink, drying her hands on a towel. "I was just thinking about your daughter. What I would have given to have known my father. Promise me you'll get involved. Be her daddy even if she's almost thirty and married."

Gretchen Newman, you're one fine lady. "I will."

"You have no idea what a difference you can make in her sense of security. And her image of God." She turned back to the sink and began scrubbing at the caramel that would have melted in the warm water if she'd given it a little time. "Maybe it's none of my business, but I need to know. . ."

Steven set the cover on the butter dish and nodded to her back. "About Jeanie?"

"Those old feelings aren't really gone, are they?" Reddened eyes turned to him.

He picked up the dish and carried it to the cupboard above the toaster. He moved the saltshaker to make room, slid in the dish, and closed the door.

"I. . .need some time to figure things out." He didn't turn around.

Behind him, the sink drained, the sprayer rinsed it. A drawer opened and closed.

Footsteps headed toward the table. From the corner of his eye he saw her unbutton the flannel shirt and lay it over the back of the chair.

"I think I'll get an early start."

⁂

It was time. The boys needed to know. Steven stuck the clean cake pan in the cupboard next to the stove and pulled out his phone. As he did, he glanced under the kitchen table. Sandals. Gretchen's sandals. She'd left in bare feet.

Lord, I handled that so wrong. He stared down at his phone and pushed a number that didn't belong to either of his sons. His friend's voice eased a bit of tension. "Burt, I need a dose of wisdom."

A low rumble met his ear. "Just happened to have read a few chapters in Proverbs this morning. What's up?"

"Gretchen."

"Oh. You didn't mention you wanted woman wisdom. Fresh out of that. Ask my daughters—I've never had much of that."

"You and me both." Steven opened the back door and walked out on the deck. The air smelled of warm damp earth. "Jeanie showed up this morning while Gretchen was here."

"And you hadn't breathed a word of this to Gretchen yet, right?"

"Right. It was all very civil until Jeanie left."

"And the questions started."

Steven stretched out on the green and tan striped hammock. "She asked me if I still had feelings for Jeanie."

"Please tell me you didn't say yes."

"I didn't say yes."

"Good."

"But I didn't say no."

In spite of his predicament, Burt's sputtering laugh made him smile. "Smooth shave, Gillette. Well, you've been looking for a way out. Looks like you found it."

"I didn't want a way out. I wanted a reprieve, a break. I just wish she'd give me enough time to figure out if I'd miss her. She's been up here at least once a month since I moved."

"Funny she didn't get that hint. Moving to Elizabeth, Illinois, wasn't exactly an upgrade from the Dallas public school system."

"I told her I wanted to get back to my roots and lead a simpler, slower lifestyle. That was the truth. I just didn't mention I wanted a quieter life, too." He pushed against the deck rail and the hammock swung. "She can be a little intense."

"And now you've got two women and you're not sure how you feel about either one. Nice, quiet life. You need to call Gretchen. Let her know it's not over, unless you want it to be. Spell it out. Women always figure they know what we're thinking. I'd bet money she thinks it's over between you two."

"Why does there have to be a 'thing' to be over? Why couldn't we just be friends and wait and see how things progress?"

"Because you're a man and she's a woman."

"I knew I could count on you for profundity."

"You don't have to thank me. Any other problems I can solve on this fine morning?"

"Yeah. You want to call my boys and let them know they've got a sister?"

The sputtering laugh resounded. "Wouldn't touch that with an eighty-foot telephone pole. But I'll pray."

❧

"I knew you'd call. I was sure I'd hear your voice before I

crossed the Mississippi. I understand your need for space."

"Thank you, Gretchen. I'm just in a bit of shock right now. I need to figure out how all this new information fits into my world."

"Everything in its place." He could hear her smile. "Now if you could just learn to dust."

He didn't even want to know if there was hidden meaning in her comment. Knowing Gretchen, it was most likely literal. He laughed. "Never. Thanks again for understanding. I'm going to go call my kids now."

"Steven?"

"Yes?"

"Can I still help with the pizza sale?"

His eyes closed. So much for space. "Of course." He didn't sigh until she hung up.

As long as the phone was in his hand, he might as well get all of his calls over and done with. Positive kid first, or negative? He'd always held to the philosophy that it was better to get the bad out of the way so you could thoroughly enjoy the good. Eat the lima beans out of the succotash first, delete the spam before reading personal e-mails.

So he'd call the half-empty son first. He punched "3" and waited for Griffin's voice. "Hello?"

"Griff. Are you in the middle of something?"

"Always. But I've got a minute. Actually, I was going to call you at lunch. Do you have plans for next weekend?"

Next weekend? Father's Day. Irrational hope sprouted and he squashed it. "Nothing special." *Why?*

"Well you do now. How'd you like a couple bums hanging out at your house?"

"A couple? You bringing a friend?" *Or. . .please God. . .a brother?*

"Toby and I are flying in Friday night."

He'd prided himself, especially in the last few years, on having mastered the art of reining in emotion. But it wasn't even noon and this was the second time he'd mopped at tears. *Softy.* "That will be"—*better than any gift money could buy*—"wonderful."

"I'll e-mail details. Hey, I have to go. Boss got up on the wrong side of the world this morning. Did you call about something in particular?"

"Nothing that can't wait until the weekend. Love you."

"Love you, too."

Happy Father's Day. . .times three.

seven

"Taste." Jeanie held out two numbered paper plates. On each was a slice of yellow cake cut in half. "Tell me which one you like the best."

"My pleasure." Lucas occupied his usual spot at the counter, staring, out of habit, at the CLOSED sign across the street.

"Wait till I lock up." Her mother walked past Lucas, locked the door, and turned off the signs, then came back to the counter and tasted both cakes.

Lucas's eyebrows huddled together in overstated concentration. "Hmm. Number one is light, buttery. Two has a stronger hint of vanilla, but could be a smidgeon sweeter. I think. . .one. Ruby? What do you—" His eyes narrowed. "Who's that?"

A knock sounded on the glass. Jeanie looked up. "What in the world is she doing here?"

Her mother unlocked the door and a girl walked in. Sixteen years old, brown hair in short pigtails covered by a triangle scarf tied at the back of her neck. She wore khaki overalls and a tan T-shirt and carried a backpack.

Jeanie ran around the end of the counter. "Taylor." She hugged her daughter's new and very bedraggled-looking sister-in-law. "Do your parents know you're here?"

Taylor shrugged out of her backpack and set it on the floor. Hazel eyes looked down at the bulging pack. "Wade's rent is paid up until the end of the month. I'm staying there."

Having met Wade's parents several times, Jeanie knew they hadn't given their blessing. "How did you get here?"

"I got a ride."

Taylor's evasiveness was all too recognizable to someone

54

who'd once made an art form out of skirting truth. A ribbon of fear looped around her chest, making her suddenly light-headed. "With someone you know?"

"Of course." Taylor's sandaled toe jabbed her pack.

Jeanie didn't buy it. "Taylor?"

The toe began kicking faster. "They were nice people."

Chills skittered along the backs of her arms. Memory ghosts whispered. "You could have been. . .hurt." She took a deep breath. "Sit down. When's the last time you ate?"

"This morning."

"I'll get you something." *And then I'll call your parents and then I'll make you talk*. She pointed to the stool two down from Lucas. "Lucas, I'd like you to meet my new son-in-law's sister, Taylor Ramsey, a fugitive from Wheaton."

"I'm not a fugitive. I'm going to take care of Wade's plants and stuff."

"Mm-hmm. Taylor, this is Lucas Zemken. He owns the jewelry store across the street."

Lucas held out his hand. "Glad to meet you, Taylor. Seems you and I have something in common."

Don't you dare tell her some yarn glorifying hitchhiking.

"What's that?"

"I was a fugitive once."

Rolling her eyes, Jeanie walked around the end of the counter. Lucas was a storyteller. Only a fraction of the tales he spun were true.

"Really?"

"Had an APB out on my sorry hide—half the sheriffs in Jo Daviess County plus a search party combing the woods and checking every abandoned building for miles around."

"What did you do? Why were you running?" Taylor's eyes widened with what appeared to be admiration. Not a good sign.

"I absconded with the contents of my mother's purse."

Jeanie glanced at her mother and both shook their heads.

Her mother leaned across the counter and put her chin in her hand. "How old were you, Lucas?"

A small bump appeared in his cheek. "I was four."

Taylor burst into giggles.

"I stole a pack of gum and knew there was a wooden spoon with my name on it, so I ran. Cops found me in my grandma's garage. Never did get that spoon. Slick, huh?" He held his hand out, palm up.

Taylor slapped his hand. "Slick."

"So what are you doing here, Taylor? Problems at home? You're honor bound to tell me since I confessed my crimes to you."

A sigh as big as she was whistled out of Taylor. "My parents are forcing me to go to church camp."

Good work, Lucas. Jeanie reached across the counter and rested her hand on Taylor's shoulder. In a no-nonsense yet gentle tone she asked, "Will you call your parents or should I?"

The girl's shoulders slumped. "I will. But first can I tell you why I came here?"

"Of course."

"I don't want to go to church camp because some of my friends are going and they're the ones that pulled me down before when I was drinking and stuff. I can't tell my parents 'cause they figure they're all good kids. And besides, I don't want to be forced to sing songs about how I believe in Jesus 'cause I don't really yet and I just want to figure it out myself on my own. Anyway, I was working for Angel on the weekends, you know, and I don't have a job until they get back and move to Chicago, so I was wondering if maybe I could work for you if you need somebody to clean the bakery or something or I could get a job somewhere else here and I was wondering if maybe I could stay with you and help you take care of Sunny until they get back." She finally stopped to breathe.

Jeanie reached into a box on the counter and pulled out a filled doughnut. "Mom, can you get a glass of milk?" It was an excuse to make eye contact.

Her mother nodded and the lines around her eyes compressed in a smile. "I'm good with it if you are." Her answer had nothing to do with a glass of milk.

Jeanie set the doughnut in front of Taylor. "As a matter of fact, we're looking for part-time help. But I warn you, I might not be as soft a boss as Angel."

Taylor grinned. "I don't think you can be too tough with a name like Dreamy." Her nose crinkled and she laughed.

Heat rose from the base of Jeanie's neck to the tips of her ears. "How did you—"

"Mr. Vandenburg was showing a high school picture of you to Angel at the wedding. It said, 'All my love forever. Dreamy' on the back. It's the coolest story in the world how you two found each other after all this time. It's like destiny, you know, like you were meant to be together and now—"

"We're not together, Taylor."

"Not yet maybe. But if I have anything to say about it. . ."

"You don't—"

A laugh popped from Lucas like a punctured balloon. He held his hand out to Taylor for another high five. "Count me in, girl." Their hands smacked. "Love is in the air."

"For sure."

※

Steven ran a damp cloth along the top of the nightstand, stared at the ridge of gray he'd collected, and tucked the cloth in his back pocket. He picked up the alarm clock. Twelve o' clock blinked in red. The clock hadn't been set since a storm had knocked out the power for an hour three weeks ago. Griff would bring his own alarm, no doubt. Satellite radio most likely—voice activated, with a built-in GPS, if such a thing existed. Griff was doing all right for himself. Steven smoothed the plaid spread on the twin bed and walked across the hall to the other guest room.

Toby, on the other hand, would show up with the Army

duffel bag he'd bought at a surplus store in Dallas six years ago when he went on a high school mission trip. In the bag would be a few of the shirts he'd taken on that trip and a couple pairs of faded jeans. And that would be just fine by him. Steven dusted the dresser, picking up the tattered Bible Promise Book Toby had been awarded in fourth grade for memorizing the Beatitudes. The book wouldn't stay on the dresser while Toby was here. He'd find it on the bedside table when his youngest son left.

He looked at another clock radio flashing twelve and glanced at his watch. The boys should be here any minute. They were meeting at the Quad City International Airport and renting a car. Which meant that this had been Griff's idea, because Griff would be paying for all of it. Which meant that he and Toby were on speaking terms and something had softened in his oldest son. Steven went downstairs and turned on the oven. Lindy's pizza crust recipe hadn't been all that tricky after all.

The front door flew open and the first sound that met his ears threatened to start those ridiculous sappy tears again. Arguing. His sons arguing. . .

Celtics versus Sonics.

Thank You, Lord.

&.

Toby pushed aside his paper plate. Sun-streaked and carefree, chin-length brown hair tumbled over the collar of his faded shirt when he shook his head. "I'm stuffed. That was good, Dad. Mom woulda been proud. Or shocked, maybe." He laughed and folded the plate in half.

On the opposite end of the table, Griffin tapped his upper and lower front teeth together. It was an unconscious gesture accompanied by a slow, steady inhale and used primarily for his brother. It meant Griff was merely tolerating the moment. Steven knew the root of his impatience. Though it had been almost four years since his mother died, he seemed to think it irreverent to speak of her in anything but somber tones. Lindy would have hated that. Steven felt an obligation to loosen the boy up.

"I think Mom would be shocked at a lot of things I'm capable of these days. I cleaned the oven a few weeks ago and—" Griff slid his chair back, but Steven didn't let it alter what he was going to say. "Wait till you see the impatiens I planted in the backyard."

"Cool."

Griff walked toward the living room, running his hand through short, gelled dark hair. When he got to the back door he stopped and bent over. "Think Mom would be proud to know you had some woman's shoes in your kitchen?" Gretchen's sandals dangled from his finger when he stood. What could so easily have been an opportunity for humor was anything but with Griff. "Whose are they?"

First of all, I'm your father and I don't need to explain. Second of all, if you don't know me well enough to know it's not what it might look like. . . "They're Gretchen's."

"I thought you moved to break it off with her." Griff's disgust was almost tangible.

Never, ever, had he breathed a word of that to his boys. Had it been that obvious that part of his motivation for changing jobs was to disentangle? "There was nothing to break off. She's an old friend."

"Of Mom's." He walked into the living room, footsteps ricocheting off the vaulted ceiling.

Toby swiveled around in his chair. "Drop it, Griff," he yelled. "Dad's a big boy. Let him have a life."

The footsteps continued up the stairs, followed by a bedroom door shutting with too much force.

So maybe tonight wasn't the best time to tell them the news.

જ

Steven woke on Saturday morning to the sound of his weed

trimmer. Griffin. Why couldn't that boy ever relax? The next sound he heard was Toby's plaster-rattling snores. How could two offspring be so night-and-day different? Same parents, same rules and advantages. Not for the first time, he reassured himself that God was in control, even when it came to his boys. The Creator of the Universe had, after all, designed Cain and Abel, Esau and Jacob, and Joseph and his brothers. And the world had survived.

Steven got up and walked into the bathroom. He turned on the shower then looked in the mirror. He'd put on some weight since Lindy died. Stress eating. He turned sideways and stared at his profile. His frame could carry a bit extra, but maybe it was time to stop with the comfort food. And exercise. Grimacing at his reflection, he pulled his T-shirt off. Definitely time to make some changes.

After breakfast.

Maybe someday his boys would join him for the Saturday morning men's prayer breakfasts at church. Toby had joined him several times, Griff never. This morning he'd be cooking for his boys—something he'd surprisingly come to enjoy when he had someone to cook for. Lindy would indeed be proud. And shocked.

After his shower he threw on khaki shorts and a polo shirt and went down to the kitchen. Six slices of French toast were browning on the electric griddle when Toby sauntered in. Flannel boxers and a T-shirt with a hole under one arm and hair sticking out every which way made him look about six instead of nineteen.

"Morning, son."

"Hey." Toby opened the refrigerator and pulled out a carton of orange juice. He swirled the contents and downed it straight from the carton. Some things never change. At least at this age he threw the empty container away instead of sticking it back in the fridge.

"You and Griff get anything settled after I went to bed?"

"I don't know. He's a mess."

"Tobe. . ." Steven warned with a look that didn't work when Toby was six and would probably have little effect now.

"Seriously. You know it, too. He needs to figure out God's the good guy in all this and quit being mad at the world."

"You realize it's always been harder for him because he remembers Mom before she got sick. Six years makes a huge difference—you grew up accepting her illness because you never knew anything else." Steven picked two eggs out of the carton and cracked them simultaneously onto the griddle, earning a thumbs-up from his son.

Toby opened three cupboards before he found the syrup bottle. "I get that. But that doesn't change the fact that he should have worked past his anger by now. Look at you. . . you're moving on with life." He nodded toward the infamous sandals. "Got a woman, even." His laugh filled the kitchen.

It wasn't exactly a conscious thought that flipped a barely warmed egg from the griddle onto his son's holey shirt. But it felt mighty good.

Toby's yelp was rewarding. But only until a slow drizzle of syrup trickled down the back of Steven's head. This time he grabbed an egg right out of the carton.

Moving at light speed, Toby found a can of whipped cream in the refrigerator. Steven's only recourse was a plate of soft butter. "You're going down, boy." He was laughing so hard he could barely utter the threat. He scooped a handful of butter just as sweet cream foamed across one eye and filled his ear.

It was at that moment Griffin walked in carrying a fruit basket. "What the. . ." His foot hit butter and Toby, thanks to years of basketball, caught the basket as Griff grabbed the edge of the table and managed to plant his backside on a chair instead of the floor.

"Smooth shave, Gillette," Steven wheezed. Burt's favorite phrase seemed the only fitting comment.

Griff glared and pulled off his shoe. Toby set the basket on the table and pulled off the cellophane. "Yum."

It wasn't an ordinary fruit basket. Cut fruit on sticks was arranged in a bowl that looked like a basketball. The bowl overflowed with grapes, cantaloupe, honeydew, daisies cut out of pineapple, and chocolate-dipped strawberries. Amid the fruit was a small Mylar balloon that said "Happy Father's Day."

Steven wiped whipped cream on his pants. "Aw, you guys. That's so cool."

"I didn't send it."

"Me neither."

Oh no.

Toby turned the balloon around. There were words scrawled on the silver back.

Oh no.

"Who's Angel?"

eight

"Did Mom know?"

"Griff, *I* didn't know."

"But did Mom know you were. . .intimate with another woman before her?"

The answer is no, but it's none of your business.

Toby's hands met to form a T. "Time out. That's Dad's business."

Thank you.

"I think we should just look at the cool part of this." Toby, raw egg still gooped on his shirt, slid two pieces of French toast onto a plate and handed it to Griffin. "We've got a big sister, bro."

"Thrilling. I suppose she's going to join us for Christmas. Maybe we can take her hunting with us at Thanksgiving."

"Maybe we should. We can do sibling bonding in a tree stand."

Griff snarled.

Lord, help. Steven refilled his coffee cup for the second time in ten minutes.

"Can we meet her?" Toby's hopeful smile once again made him look like a little kid.

"She's on her honeymoon."

"Let's call her."

"I only have her office number." *But I could get her cell number from her mother.* And then it dawned on him—he had Wade's cell number. But what kind of guy would interrupt his buddy on his honeymoon? "Are you serious?"

"As a heart attack." Toby smirked at his brother. "I want to officially welcome her to the family."

Steven had locked horns with his oldest son almost since his birth. His reaction to Griff's scowl probably wasn't what a God-honoring man should be feeling. But the boy needed some shaking up. "Okay. I'll get her number."

Saturday morning. . .would Jeanie be at the bakery? He'd start there. He reached for the phone.

"You can eat first." Toby held a plate out to him.

"Yeah, I suppose I can."

Since when did making a phone call sound better than French toast?

&

Jeanie opened the door to her apartment and set her purse on the table with a *thud*. She had forty-five minutes to shower and change. . .everything. Her clothes, her attitude, everything.

Why had she just said yes to something guaranteed to make her feel like a butterfly on a pinning block? Steven had asked for Angel's number, she'd given it, and the next thing she knew she was agreeing to lunch at Fried Green Tomatoes with him and his sons.

Awkward.

He'd said his boys wanted to learn more about Angel. She'd tried to get out of it. She'd suggested they wait and talk to Angel herself. But Steven had countered that the boys wouldn't be back until Thanksgiving. The man had been downright pushy. And she'd caved.

As she peeled off flour-dusted clothes, unbraided her hair, and let the shower massage pound her head, she prayed. Fighting God was senseless. She knew that from way too much experience. But what was He doing? Why now, when she was on the verge of finally figuring out what she wanted from life, had He brought Steven back into it? If the Divine plan for her had included Steven, why hadn't it worked out years ago?

Because you didn't let it.

She squeezed the shampoo too hard. A clear green pool filled the palm of her hand. She rubbed it in, scrubbing hard until suds fell to her feet in globs.

What's this all about, Lord? What are You trying to show me? The shower massaged her scalp, foam slid down her shoulders and back. *And why am I having lunch with Steven?* She didn't believe for a minute his sons were all that anxious to meet his old girlfriend. . .the mother of their half sister.

In spite of the steam rising around her, she shivered. Half sister. Her pulse did a tiny skip. Angel had brothers. What if they wanted an ongoing relationship with her? Angel would have the siblings she'd always longed for, the father she'd written about in her journal. *That's a good thing.* But if things didn't work out between her and Steven. . .and if Steven ever remarried. . .

She cranked the faucet. The water turned icy. Good for closing pores. . .and freezing thoughts.

❧

"What are you going to school for, Toby?"

Blue eyes that looked eerily like Angel's sparkled. "I have absolutely no idea."

Jeanie laughed. She felt immediately comfortable with Steven's younger son. "I love your honesty. Don't rush it." She took a piece of bread from the basket Steven held out to her. "And I practice what I preach—I'm actually just now figuring out what I want to be when I grow up."

"What do you want to do?"

"Like your father, I want to teach."

"Awesome." Blond highlights danced in his hair as he nodded. "It's a good calling."

"It is. What makes you passionate, Toby?"

"God. People. God changing people. I'm wondering if I should just drop out of school and go on the mission field."

"What?" Steven scrunched his napkin in a ball. "Where did this come from? You are not dropping out of school."

"He might as well." Griffin, who had been sitting like a stone statue to her left, shrugged. "His grades aren't good enough to get him into graduate school."

Steven's eyes closed and opened in a slow blink. Jeanie sensed that tension between his sons was something he was used to, and that things might escalate quickly if someone didn't do something. As if on cue, the waitress set a plate of the restaurant's signature dish in the center of the table— breaded and sautéed sliced green tomatoes, sprinkled with mozzarella and parmesan cheese. Jeanie breathed a sigh for Steven. "Have you ever had these, Griffin?"

"No."

Conversation with this guy wasn't going to be easy. But a woman who could cover a cake with a hundred and forty-six handmade frosting roses, as she'd done just this morning, had the patience to make a stubborn man talk. "Your dad says you work in Tacoma. . .for a paper company?"

Ouch. If looks could wound, she'd be bleeding. So evidently he didn't work for a paper company.

After the laser look, Griffin blinked at exactly the same speed his father had moments ago. "I work for Richlite Company. We manufacture paper-based fiber composites used for architectural, recreational, and industrial applications. All of our materials are manufactured out of environmentally sustainable resources harvested from certified managed forests." The last three words were articulated as if Jeanie were just off the boat from a non-English-speaking country.

Okay then. She could feel Steven's embarrassment radiating across the table. But God was so clearly at work in this moment, it took all her willpower to restrain the smile tempting her lips. She copied Griffin's posture, folding her hands and leaning forward. "Was it difficult getting the NSF certification for using your product in the food service industry? I can't imagine the trial and error that went into creating a tabletop surface that's water, temperature, and bacteria resistant *and* satisfies the growing demand for green products. How long did it take to perfect that?"

Surprise registered ever so slightly, but Griffin covered it smoothly. "You're familiar with our product."

"Familiar would be an understatement. I *dream* of your product." Was she slathering it a little thick? A quick glance at Steven confirmed his approval. "I'm competing in a contest in which a bakers table with a Richlite top is part of the grand prize." She pointed a piece of garlic bread at him. "I intend to win."

Griffin Vanderburg actually smiled. Jeanie felt like she'd just swung a hammer and rung the bell at the county fair. *Bong!*

"Let's pray." Steven's eyes glistened with mirth as he bent his head. "Father, thank You for gathering us together and for the food You have provided. We acknowledge Your presence. Help us glorify You in all that we say and do. Amen."

"Amen." Jeanie automatically looked straight at Steven as he ended the prayer. The look he returned unraveled her.

Turning away, she looked at Griff and then Toby. "I imagine it was quite a shock for you two to learn you had a. . .that your father has a daughter." In the space between pulse beats where she'd almost said "sister," a floodlight flashed on. Her breath caught in her throat. "I. . .owe you both an apology. I was so sure"—all her excuses seemed suddenly empty, worthless—"I was doing the right thing by not upsetting your father's life all these years. I never thought about him having other children and what it would mean to them to have a. . ."

Sister. A fresh wave of realization and regret slammed into her. The blow felt physical. *Oh, Lord, what did I do to these boys? To Angel? They should have known each other all these years. . . .* Her next breath shuttered in her chest. "I'm sorry." Her hand closed around the handle of her purse. "Excuse me." She ran to the bathroom. The stall door closed as a sob pushed against the hand she held over her mouth.

This wasn't like her. She wasn't an unstable person. *Stop this*. She ripped a piece of toilet paper and blew her nose. *Get a grip. You can't change the past. What's done is done.* Her cheeks welcomed a splash of cold water as she rehearsed a return to the table without the drama of her exit. Steven said the boys wanted to hear about Angel. That's what she was here for.

Fresh lipstick did little to enhance her blotchy face, but it was all she had to work with. *What's done is done. You can't change the past.* Reciting her mantra, she stepped into the hall... and almost into Steven.

The compassion in his eyes brought the tears precariously near the surface again. *Breathe. Again.* She smiled, sure her casual act wasn't convincing. "Sorry about that." She kept her voice light, her tone implying she was just having one of those female moments men laugh about.

"Let's walk outside for a minute."

"I'm fine, really." The last thing that would help her lack of composure was a minute alone with those eyes.

"Come on." He held out his hand as a waiter walked by. She'd look foolish if she didn't take it. She put her hand in his.

He'd put on weight, grown a beard, his hair had grayed and thinned, but the feel of his hand hadn't changed. Strange that she could remember the sensation so clearly. Her thumb found the scar on his index finger. The scar she'd caused.

Steven winked and reached for the door handle. "It's still there. Reminds me of you."

The air was too warm to take the heat from her face. *Keep it light.* "Did it ever remind you to forgive me?" She cringed. Her mouth tasted suddenly sour. *What a stupid thing to say.*

He turned to her as they walked past the window where Toby and Griffin could easily see them. "That's what I want to talk to you about." His eyes seemed shadowed, darkened by the furrow between his eyebrows.

Not here, Steven. Let's talk about how you straightened the picture in my paper cutter. . .too late. And how I wrapped your finger in my scarf and you teased you'd never forgive me. . .right before you kissed me the first time.

She tried to extract her hand, but he didn't let go. "Steven. . ."

They passed Durty Gurt's, and Steven pulled her into an empty lot between two buildings. Letting go of her hand, he faced her. "I owe you an apology. I don't even know how to say it. But I need you to know. . ." He took her hand and pressed it against his chest. His heart hammered against her palm. "I need you to believe how sorry I am for what I put you through. I should have been the strong one. I should have had enough self-control for both of us. I've been angry the past two weeks, putting all this on you, but it's my fault you got pregnant, my fault you had to raise Angel alone."

Don't do this, Steven. Tears wouldn't listen to her commands to retreat. She looked up the street, wanting desperately to run. "Steven. . ."

"Can you forgive me?"

"I never blamed you. Never. We were both"—*so much in love*—"so young."

"I know," he whispered.

"Life goes on."

The hint of a smile graced his lips. "Can *we?*"

"If we leave the past behind."

"Okay." He released her hand. "Let's start the future with lasagna." The end of the finger with the scar touched the tip of her nose.

And made leaving the past behind impossible.

nine

"Mom? You'll never believe who called me."

"Just a minute, honey." Jeanie slipped the open phone in her apron pocket, set a ball of blue fondant on the dented stainless-steel table, and covered it with a towel. Brushing her hands on her apron, she took a shaky breath, smiled, and picked up the phone again. "I bet I can guess. Toby Vandenburg?"

"Yes! Mom, he's so sweet and funny and. . ." Angel sniffed and blew her nose in Jeanie's ear. "I feel like I've known him all my life. He's going to fly to Chicago to meet us as soon as we get home."

"That's won—"

Taylor walked in from the bakery, waving at her. "You've got company," she whispered.

"Just a minute, Ange." She held the phone against her chest. "Can't my mother handle it?"

Pigtails jiggled as the girl laughed. "Not hardly. It's your long-lost love."

"Tell him to wait in my office."

She lifted the phone to her ear. "That's wonderful. Wade and Toby will get along great."

"I hope so. Can't you just picture Christmas with all of us together?"

"Yes." *But I can also picture you with your new family. . .and me alone.* "Honey, I need to get going. Someone's waiting in my office."

"Okay. Room service will be here with our breakfast in a minute anyway. I love you and I'll e-mail pictures soon. Send us pictures of your cake when it's done. Hey, tell Taylor to call sometime, okay?"

"Sure."

"I want to tell her all about her brother's new brother-in-law."

And how fun it will be when we're all together for Christmas.

Jeanie swiped at a tear, said good-bye to her daughter, and slammed the phone onto the table.

❧

His beard was gone.

Jeanie grabbed onto the handle of her office door. He looked so much younger. "You. . .you shaved."

"Thought it was time for a change. Are you busy?"

"A little. I'm working with fondant. It's not very forgiving."

"Unlike me."

Why, oh why, had she chosen that word? Steven grinned. Dimples materialized.

Oh, those dimples. . . "I'm. . ." She swallowed. Her throat felt dusted with cake flour. "I'm working on the cake for the contest. I'm almost done."

"Can I see?"

Anything to get out of the room that seemed to shrink around them. She led him to the kitchen and pointed toward a two-foot-high cake with five layers in graduating sizes. Two layers were Wedgwood blue, three were white. She'd been working since before dawn on the painstaking task of forming tiny flowers and ribbons to cover it.

Steven gasped. "Wow. It's unbelievable. It looks like my grandmother's dishes."

"I got the idea from the china Angel and Wade picked out. The pattern is called Harmony."

"Nice name." The dimples came into view again.

"The one for the contest will have a lot more flowers and ribbons. I'm donating this one to the Veteran's home. I'll make another in a few weeks. The judges want pictures before the contest so Lucas is going to photograph."

"You never heard from Gretchen?"

"No. I didn't really expect. . ."

Steven nodded.

"And then I should be able to make the whole thing by heart. We can't use a recipe or pictures for the contest."

"Impressive. Can I watch you work?"

How could she possibly steady her hand to place miniature ribbons in exactly the right places with him watching? She shrugged, embarrassed in a way she hadn't been in years. She walked over to the sink and began washing her hands. "I'll have to ask you to wear a hairnet." That would make any guy run.

"It'll enhance my new look."

She dried her hands and took a hairnet and apron out of the cupboard and handed them to him. He tied the apron and stretched the net over his hair. Scarred finger pressed against his chin, he did a Shirley Temple–style curtsy.

Jeanie laughed and sat down. She motioned toward a wheeled stool on the opposite side of the table. What was he doing here anyway? "I just talked to Angel. She and Toby really clicked." She fought the image that popped in her head—Angel and her brothers and father posing in front of a Christmas tree. Without her.

"It sounds that way. Toby's planning a trip to see them next month. I imagine he's assuming his spineless father will kick in the cost of a ticket."

"And will he?"

"Of course."

She looked up from the fondant warming in her hand and forgot what she was about to say. Wedgwood. Steven's eyes were Wedgwood blue. She cleared her throat and picked up a rolling pin. "You're a good father."

"Thank you. It hasn't been easy. As you saw, I have one child who brings sunlight into a room and one who sucks it out."

She set the rolling pin on the fondant and began flattening it. "And a third who is all or nothing. . .sometimes black, sometimes white." Her voice came out as hushed as her thoughts.

"Does it bother you that we want to be part of Angel's life?"

"No." She picked up a cutting tool and cut a thin, wavy strip.

"If I were you I'd be hurting right now."

He could still see through her. She used to love the feeling, now it made her nervous. "I'm happy for her."

The room filled with silence until a timer buzzed. Taylor walked in, smiled her smirky smile, and put on oven mitts.

Steven waved. "How are you, Taylor? Has this lady got you working hard?"

Taylor pulled a pan of twenty lemon poppy seed muffins out of an oven. "I love the work. I was sure I wanted to be a party planner like Angel, but now I think I want to own my own bakery."

Steven laughed. "First get yourself through high school."

A sputter answered him. Taylor took out a pan of Morning Glory muffins and set them on a rack. "What I really need is a tutor for English." She walked toward Steven. "Do you ever tutor, Mr. Vandenburg?"

You little sneak. "Mr. Vandenburg is the school principal, Taylor. He doesn't tutor."

"You would, wouldn't you, Mr. Vandenburg, if it included a home-cooked meal? Ruby's going to teach me how to make Polish food and I need someone to practice on."

The dimples did an encore. "I don't really see how I could turn that down."

"Cool. Thursday night then. Six o'clock." The oven mitts flew onto a counter and the girl with the pigtails bounced out of the room.

Steven's lips pressed together. "A baking, party-planning, little matchmaker is what that girl's going to be."

"Not the subtle type, is she?"

"No. But I like the way she operates. She just gave me a segue."

"Into what?" A swarm of grasshoppers took up residence in Jeanie's stomach.

"Into asking you out. My teachers gave me a gift certificate for *Mark Twain and the Laughing River.* Have you seen it?"

"No. I've heard it's fun." A date with Steven. Could she? Should she? Could the demons of three years of her life stay sealed in her memory and never escape to undo what seemed to be starting all over again? Would Steven keep his eyes on their present and future and leave the past behind? She'd never know unless she said yes. "I'd love to see it. . .with you."

છે

Steven drove into the driveway of the little white cottage feeling like a trespasser. He'd been here just once, and then only to throw pebbles at an upstairs window. To wake the girl who'd fallen asleep when she'd promised to meet him.

He parked, wiped his hands on his pant legs, and picked up the spray of white carnations and small pink roses wrapped in waxy green paper. He got out and stared up at the dormer window, wondering if little stones still lingered on the window frame. Transported, he hummed the theme song from *I Dream of Jeannie,* just like he'd done when she'd snuck out the back door in bare feet that night, hair tousled from sleep. . .and rushed into his arms.

Ruby opened the door for him, interrogating him with her gaze as if he'd arrived in a souped-up car to whisk her daughter to the prom. After a nervous moment, she smiled, mischief sparking in gray eyes. "Come in."

"Thank you." He handed her the flowers. *I come in peace.*

"You should give these to the cook. . .or the person you really came to see." The spark brightened.

He shook his head. "These are for my lovely hostess."

The tiny woman laughed. "Smart man. You have to get by me to get to my daughter. This time." She winked and ushered him into a steamy, heavenly scented kitchen.

Jeanie stood with her back to him, chopping vegetables. She

turned, smiled shyly, and nudged Taylor. "Your tutor's here."

The girl turned around and waved at him with a butcher knife. "Hey, Mr. Vandenburg. Wanna help?"

Slipping out of his sport jacket, he unbuttoned one sleeve. "If it will help us get to your tutoring quicker."

Taylor's mouth opened. "That was just a joke." She gave a nervous laugh. "You knew that."

Rolling up his sleeve, Steven stepped next to Jeanie. For the briefest moment he let his hand rest on her elbow. "Hi."

"Hi." Her shyness was becoming.

He picked up a carrot peeler and aimed it at Taylor. "Maybe to you it was a joke. Teaching's serious business to me." He pointed to a stained recipe card. "*Golabki.* Sounds delicious." He wrinkled his nose.

Jeanie laughed. "Cabbage rolls."

"Is that what I smell?" *And what's that other smell?* Sweet, with a hint of vanilla. The woman beside him smelled like warm vanilla custard.

Taylor nodded. "It's in the oven."

He picked up another card. "*Adass.* What's that?"

"Vegetable salad."

He nodded. "So, Taylor, what if I wanted to make this recipe plus half again as much, how much mayo—"

"Huh-uh. You're not a math teacher anyway, and you know why I said the tutoring thing." A gleam lit her eyes. "The only math you guys should be doing is you-plus-you-equals-two!" With that, she hightailed it out the back door with the dog, giggling as she ran.

Jeanie sucked in her cheeks, widened her eyes, then released her cheeks with a popping sound—a face she'd once used just to make him laugh. Her shyness seemed to fade without the prying teenage eyes.

Without thinking, his arm slid around her waist. She didn't resist. "How can I help?" He whispered.

She lifted her face to him, the silly look gone. "It helps. . .

just that you're here."

His knees felt suddenly wobbly. Leaning down, he brushed his lips across her hair. "It helps me, too."

❧

It was after ten on Friday night when *Mark Twain and the Laughing River* ended. As they walked out of the Trolley Depot Theater, Steven hummed a tune from the show and tucked her hand in his. They walked between two red and green trolleys. As Jeanie looked up at the green and gold Trolley Times clock, Steven grabbed her hands and swung her around. "Oh. . .the rhythm of the river is the rhythm of life," he sang. "And dum-de-dum-de something. . .the Mighty Mississippi is the heartbeat of the land. . . ."

Jeanie laughed and joined in, conscious that a stream of tourists heading toward their bus stared at them. When Steven stopped, she impulsively hugged him. "Thank you. That was wonderful."

"My singing or dancing?"

"The show." She laughed again and reluctantly pulled her arms away.

On the way home, they talked about their favorite parts of Jim Post's portrayal of Mark Twain. The drive took only minutes, making her wish they'd decided to walk. She put her hand on the handle of the car door. "Thank you. . .again."

Steven reached across the seat and held out his hand, palm up. She slid her left hand into it. His eyes held hers. The years, the separation, all she'd done to survive, faded in the intensity of his gaze. Leaning toward her, he touched his lips to hers.

She closed her eyes, felt the warmth of his lips, and kissed him back. Too soon, he pulled away, brushed his knuckles across her cheek, and reached for the door handle. His eyes stayed on hers. "Thank *you*."

ten

"I could watch you all day." Steven leaned on one elbow, a white hairnet sitting at a rakish angle on his head. His smile warmed her more than the heat rising from the fryer.

He'd been watching her for almost an hour as she mixed dough for angel wings and ran it through the sheeter. With hands that moved with practiced speed, she took one end of a flat, rectangular piece of dough and pulled it through the slit near the opposite end. She reached for a box of latex gloves. "See? Easy." She pulled out a pair of gloves. "It's time to put you to—"

Taylor swung into the room, one hand hanging on to the door frame by the fingertips. "There's a man here to see you, Jeanie, and we're almost out of"—she took a huge breath—"*okręgly chleb kartoflany.*"

Laughing, Jeanie stood, grabbed a towel, and wiped her hands as she walked toward the doorway. "I'll be right back."

Taylor shadowed her like a lost puppy. "Did I get it right? Did I say Polish potato bread?"

"It was perfect." She set the towel on the end of the counter. "I can't say it that good mysel—"

The man at the counter wore a black shirt. His black eyes zeroed in on her. "Misty. I was just passing through."

From behind, Taylor gripped her sleeve. "Who's Misty? The guy's creepy," she whispered.

With icy fingers, Jeanie patted the girl's hand. "Go keep Mr. Vandenburg company."

"But—"

"*Now.*" She stared at the man and tried to block out his

name. The name she'd known him by wasn't Denny. "What do you want?"

"I'm managing the Mississippi Moon Bar at Diamond Jo's. Starting a little business on the side, and I just happen to have a job opening for someone with your. . .experience. Val always said you were the best. 'Persuasive girl,' he used to say." He fingered the pencil mustache. "Pay's way better than it was back in the day."

"I'm not interested." She pulled her shoulders back and forced herself to engage the evil black eyes.

"Then maybe I'll settle for just a little of your time."

"Get out of here, Damon. Get out and don't come back, or I'll get a restraining order."

"For what? For walking in here and offering you a job?" Ape hands landed flat on the counter and he leaned forward. "You know, Misty girl, everybody that's important to me knows what I did in Reno, and it's way too late for me to pay for it." One eyebrow rose into his dyed hair. "Can you say the same? How old's that daughter of yours now?" He laughed and walked to the door. "Think about it. . .*Jeanie*."

The door closed behind him. He walked across the street to a black car with the top down. Jeanie's legs buckled and she grabbed the counter. Her breath came in ragged gasps. Her vision narrowed. Bending over, she willed herself not to faint. She couldn't let Steven see her like—*Steven*.

Everybody that's important to me knows what I did in Reno, and it's way too late for me to pay for it. Can you say the same?

Picking up the towel, she twisted it until her knuckles whitened. Pulling her shoulders back, she forced her trembling legs to carry her into the back room.

Steven looked up, Wedgewood eyes crinkling at the corners. "Everything okay? You look kind of—"

"Taylor, go watch the front."

Eyes fixed on the towel in her hands, she waited for Taylor to leave. "I'm. . .getting a migraine. I think I'll call Sue and see if she can come in." She couldn't look at him, couldn't hold up under the concern in his eyes. "Maybe you should go home." *Please.*

He stood and walked to her. His hands took her elbows. "What just happened out there?"

"Nothing. . .it's just. . ." She pulled away, but he didn't let go. "Life is complicated for both of us right now. I've got the contest coming up and you've got Gretchen and—"

"How in the world, after the time we've spent together this week, can you think for a moment—"

"She's in love with you."

His hands dropped. "Who was the man out there? Is there someone else?"

It was her only chance to turn him away. If he thought there was someone else. . . She started to nod, but couldn't follow through. "No. There's no one else. It's just. . .not working. We have fun together, but it's like we're trying to re-create the past. We're not the same people we used to be, Steven. Life goes on. I want to travel and teach and see the world. This just isn't a good time for me right now."

"You're not making any sense. Something happened out there." He reached toward her. "Talk to me, Jeanie. Whatever it is—"

"It's me. That's all. I shouldn't have led you on. It just suddenly came clear—I have to focus on the contest. I can't have any distractions right now."

Ripping off the hairnet, he stood. "You're honestly telling me your long shot at Paris is more important than us? You'd give up any possibility of us being together, being a family, just to see the Eiffel Tower?" He threw the net at her. "I could afford to take you to Paris every year. . .several times a year." He walked toward the door. "Or is it Paris with *me* that's the problem? Maybe you've got someone else in mind—"

"Stop it, Steven."

He brushed past her, bumping her shoulder, then turned.

"I'm not a groveler, Jeanie. I just want to be sure I'm clear on what you're saying. When you say 'right now,' does that mean things might change in the future?"

The towel slipped from her fingers and hit the table. "Let's just be content with things the way they were, Steven."

❧

Content? Not a chance.

Steven threw a steak on the grill with all the finesse of a farm boy tossing a hay bale. A second slab of meat joined it with the same snap of his wrist. He'd already tenderized the chunks to within a half inch of their lives.

"Anybody home?" Burt's voice came from somewhere near the back door.

"Out here. Help yourself to a soda."

Through the screen, he heard the refrigerator open and close, then the freezer. Burt stepped onto the deck with a glass in one hand and his Bible in the other. "Smells good."

"You should probably take over. Your supper is taking the brunt of my frustration."

"Sit down and relax then. Only have to take the moo out of it for me. You want yours hot pink, right?"

Steven did half of what he was told, sitting on the edge of the picnic table bench like a hawk ready for flight. "Relax" wasn't in his repertoire tonight. "You know me well. Why can't I find a woman just like you, Burt?"

"You like 'em mean, ugly, and tattooed, huh?"

"I'd take mean and ugly if I found one who made sense."

"So you think it's a no go, huh?"

The bottom of Steven's glass thunked on the bench. "A week ago she came this close to saying she'd never fallen out of love with me." His scarred index finger paralleled his thumb. "I know she's feeling something—it's written all over her."

"But you gotta take her at her word. Can't force it."

"I don't know if I've got what it takes to wait around."

"So don't."

"Don't what?"

Burt stabbed a steak and flipped it over. Juices spit into the coals. "Don't wait. She's not the only trout in the sea. All you gotta do is get down on one knee and you got a good woman ready to wash your socks and warm your bed. If you keep waiting on the bird in the tree, you're going to lose the goose in your hand."

Steven's chest rose. An exhale billowed his cheeks. "Maybe you're right. It doesn't feel right, but that doesn't mean it isn't." Just because he didn't believe the finality of Jeanie's answer didn't make it any less true to her. "Gretchen's a good woman. A wonderful person. We have fun together."

Burt nodded. "Life ain't perfect. If you wait around for perfect, you miss the whole shebang. You don't want to spend the rest of your life. . ."

As Burt lectured, Steven rocked—the hammock. . .and his little corner of the world. "Guess it doesn't pay to sit around and mope until she comes up with an answer that makes sense."

"Now you're talkin'."

"Better to move in the wrong direction than not move at all."

Burt stopped, steak suspended in midair. "Now you're scaring me."

"Well. . .not necessarily wrong direction. . .but if I can't have the best, it's better to have something." Once again.

Burt nodded. "And a little competition can bring a woman to her senses faster 'n a bucket o' Gatorade."

❦

Hush, baby, hush. Shh. . .Angel. Just take this like a good girl. It's sweet, like a grape sucker. Please, baby. Take it and we'll go bye-bye. This time we'll do it—

A single knock. The door creaked. A silver tray. *Bread and water today, Misty girl. Bread and water for girls who break the rules. But I can get you something more. Anything you want. Ice cream? French fries? All you have to do. . .*

Angel tugged. *Stay here by Mommy.* Weak hands grasped nothing but air. *Come here, Angel. Now. Please.*

Fre-fries? Wide blue eyes pleaded, red-gold curls bounced as she ran to the man with the evil laugh.

Come to Damon, Angel baby. Damon has treats. The parrot arm stretched out. . .

"Angel! Stop!"

Sweat soaked, heart banging her chest wall, Jeanie sat up, fumbled for the light that would banish the dream. The clock read 2:52.

Throwing off damp covers, she swung her legs over the edge of the bed and stood. Skin cold and clammy, she struggled into her robe and walked through the living room to the kitchen, flipping on lights as she passed.

She opened the fridge, took out a carton of milk, and filled a cup. As she set it in the microwave, chills shook her. *God, what should I do?*

He couldn't hurt her anymore. Not physically. She would get a restraining order if he showed up again. But any legal action would require explanation, would loose the specters of her past. *Everybody that's important to me knows what I did in Reno, and it's way too late for me to pay for it. Can you say the same?*

Her mother, Angel. . .the truth would shatter their image of her, would hurt the bakery's reputation. Steven. . .a school principal couldn't be associated with someone like her. Once again, she had to hide the truth to protect his future.

Doubts hummed like the drone of the microwave. If they knew the truth, her past would have no hold on her. Damon would have no power over her. But she could lose her daughter.

The microwave beeped. She took out her cup and slammed the door so hard it bounced open. Telling Angel was not an option.

The truth will set you free.

Not this time.

Turning on the television for background noise, she dragged herself to the shower and went through her morning routine robotlike. When she bent over to blow-dry her hair, her arms ached from tension. The weight of the past two days exerted a physical pull. *Lord, be my strength, my guide. Show me what to do. I've lost Steven. . . .* Her chest shuddered with the next breath. *I can't lose Angel.* Over the rush of warm air, she heard the phone.

Only her mother would call at twenty to four in the morning. She flipped open her phone. "Morning."

"Jeanie? It's Steven."

The heat drained from her shower-warmed body. "Hi." Her voice was barely understandable.

"I couldn't sleep. I knew you'd be up." A long sigh followed. "I said I wouldn't grovel, but I guess I'm not a man of my word. I haven't got anything to lose, have I?"

He waited, as if wanting an answer to his rhetorical question. She couldn't speak.

"I promise I won't make a habit of this. Just hear me out."

"Steven. . ." Her eyes smarted with hot tears. "Please. . ."

He took a sharp inhale. "I know you're afraid. I'm not exactly sure why. You keep talking about how much we've changed. Of course we have, but what if we'd be even better together because we're older and wiser? What would it hurt to give it a try?"

Each word slashed like a blade. She couldn't listen to any more. "You have Gretchen. You have a good li—"

"I don't believe for a minute you have no feelings for me. I've seen it in your eyes. What are you so afrai—"

Her phone slammed shut.

Telling Steven was not an option.

eleven

Lucas locked the jewelry store door from the inside and turned over the CLOSED sign. He pulled tinted shades over the windows and gestured toward a stool in front of the diamond case. "I charge two Morning Glory muffins and a turnover for each counseling session."

"Deal." Jeanie eased her tired body onto the seat and rested her arms on cool glass. Beneath tiny lights, the gems in the showcase shot brilliant prismatic flashes. "Diamonds are depressing."

His mouth twisted to one side. One white-tinged eyebrow tented. "Only for those who wish they had one."

"For this I'm forking over muffins?"

"You're here for pearls of wisdom. No guarantee they'll be pain-free." He opened a small half door and walked behind the counter. Taking a stool across from her, he folded his arms across his chest. "I won't push you for details, sweet pea, but I'm having a hard time believing you're capable of doing anything so bad he couldn't forgive you." His voice grew as soft as the velvet under the diamonds. "It's just not in you to do anything unforgivable."

Muscles in her belly contracted, pulling away from her blouse. "I did things. . ." She stared at a huge square-cut diamond. "You said you had something to tell me."

He rubbed the end-of-day stubble on his chin. "I. . .ran into Steven."

Her hands laced together on the counter. "Where? What did he say?"

Lucas simply looked at her, as if deciding whether or not to answer. After a moment he reached toward his back pocket and pulled out his wallet. "You accused me awhile back of being too chicken to try love."

"I was only—"

"I know. I wasn't offended, but I want to set the record straight." He took out a picture—a young woman, blond hair tumbling over her shoulders.

"She's beautiful."

"Her father was a multimillionaire. We met at a gem show and had a wild, romantic summer. And then *she* proposed and ruined everything. I couldn't see myself fitting into her world and I knew she'd be miserable in this little town, so I skipped the country. Spent a year with my grandparents in Wales to get over her." His eyes glistened with a faraway look. "About ten years ago I ran into her. She was married. . . to a very wealthy, very well-known man. Just like I thought she should be." Lucas shook his head and stared over her shoulder. "He was also a workaholic and an alcoholic who changed mistresses like most men change socks." His eyes bored into hers. "You know what she said to me? She said, 'I had one chance at happiness in my life and you took it away.'"

"Lucas. . ."

"If I'd believed her when she said she'd be happy here for the rest of her life, both our lives would have turned out so different." A sad smile bent his lips. "This little talk isn't about me. It's about you giving up your chance. . .and Steven's." He patted her hand. "Let him be the one to decide if he can accept whatever it is you did. Talk to him. . .and I mean *soon*."

❧

Holding the popcorn bag by one corner, Jeanie walked to the couch and picked up the remote. She'd rented *Australia*—a long, engrossing movie to get lost in. A drama to help her forget her own.

For three weeks she'd thrown herself into preparations for the contest, coming home only to sleep, leaving no unstructured time to dwell on "what ifs." If practice truly made perfect, she had the cake trophy in her pocket already. She'd tweaked her recipe and perfected her techniques until she could pipe petals and twist curlicues in her sleep.

If she actually ever slept. Stifling a yawn, she clicked PLAY. She hadn't slept more than three hours at a stretch since Damon showed up. He hadn't returned, but she had no illusions he was gone for good. The knowledge floated through every nightmare.

And Steven visited her few good dreams.

He hadn't called again. She knew him well enough to know he wouldn't, but that knowledge hadn't brought closure to her thoughts. How was he handling things? Did he have friends, a support system? *Let it go.* How Steven dealt with it wasn't her responsibility. Life was no different for either of them now than it had been before Angel's wedding. They'd both dealt with loss and loneliness. They could do it again.

Below her, the garage door opened. She walked to the window, parted the burgundy drape, and watched her mother roll the garbage can down to the curb. An unexpected sadness tightened her throat. Her mother had been widowed for twenty-one years. She had a daughter and granddaughter and dozens of friends who would be there for her as she grew older. But it wasn't the same as a husband who could share your memories, recognize your needs before you spoke them. Growing old would be lonely without—

Stop it! She closed the curtain and opened the popcorn bag, but the smell that wafted out only darkened her mood. Movie theaters, circuses, trips to the zoo—popcorn should be shared.

She shoved a handful into her mouth. She'd go nuts with thoughts like that. She pulled a cake decorating magazine from a basket next to the recliner and leafed through it. *I have things to do, places to go.*

What about after those things? After the contest, the teaching, the trips to New York and Paris. What about being her mother's age, pushing the garbage to the curb and returning to an empty house? She pictured Lucas, living alone, running a business alone, all because he hadn't taken a chance at happiness.

Steven. . . A surge of longing weakened her knees. His eyes. . . the way he'd looked at her when they stood in the empty lot. . . the way he'd touched her cheek. . . She couldn't think of anyone else she'd rather grow old with.

She reached toward the phone for the millionth time in three weeks. *Let him be the one to decide if he can accept whatever it is you did. Talk to him. . .and I mean soon.*

What if he *could* understand she'd had no choice? What if he could move beyond the horror of the truth? Steven's words nestled into her thoughts—*I haven't got anything to lose, have I?* She picked up the phone.

But what if he couldn't? She set it down. What if she told him everything and he walked away? It wouldn't be any worse than it was now. A groan of frustration echoed off the walls. This was the kind of behavior that sent people to padded cells.

Let him be the one to decide. Her hand inched toward it again. "Okay! I'll call hi—"

It rang.

She lurched away from it. Then, with jittery fingers, snatched it off the trunk. Maybe it was Steven. Maybe God was getting rid of her "what ifs" for good, taking the decision out of her hands. "Hello?"

"Jeanie? This is Gretchen Newman."

Gretchen? "Hi." Her brain bogged. "G—good to hear from you."

"Do you have a minute?"

"Yes. I was just going to sit down to watch a movie." *Or call Steven and tell him everything.* "It can wait." She rubbed her hand over her eyes and tried to focus her thoughts.

"Good. I just got off the phone with a chef friend from Indianapolis. Cookbook stuff, you know. Anyway, he mentioned he was entered in the Grégoire Pâtisserie contest and of course

I thought of you and how I'd offered to take pictures. So I was wondering. . .you're still helping with the pizza sale next weekend, right?"

Maybe. If I find the guts to make that call. "No. I won't be able to after all."

"That's what Steven thought. But I've made up my mind to persuade you. I'd really love it if you'd come and help, and I have an idea. It turns out I'll be in the Midwest all week, taking puddle jumpers all over the place. If the timing works out for you, I could spend a couple of days with you and then we could drive to Chicago together and I'll book a flight out of O'Hare on Sunday night."

Jeanie let out a quiet sigh. "That's so nice of you, but"—*but being around Steven would kill me*—"I really don't think I could affor—"

"I wouldn't charge you, silly! Photography isn't work for me, it's passion. It would be fun."

It would be free. For professional pictures at no charge she could spend two days avoiding Steven, couldn't she? She had to get used to being in the same room with him. Once Angel and Wade got home there would be times they'd have to be together. Maybe going to Chicago would give her a natural opportunity to talk to him, to give him a chance to decide. . . "Thank you." She said it before she could come up with an excuse to refuse. "You have no idea how much this means to me. And the timing would be perfect."

"Great. I'll be there on Wednesday afternoon, and we can head to Chicago with Steven on Friday."

With Steven? Her hand clenched around the phone.

"I'm staying at the Hilton and Towers. You can bunk with me. Do you have room for me at your place? A couch would be great. If not, I'll get my usual room at the. . ." Gretchen rattled on, oblivious to Jeanie's panic.

"We have room." Taylor wouldn't mind two nights on the couch.

"Wonderful. You know, I just had this feeling about you when we met. Like we were soul sisters, you know. I can't wait till we can see each other all the time. I won't have to work, so once I get that house clean and organized I'll have tons of free time. We'll have to plan a weekly thing—we can take turns having lunch at each other's houses when I'm up there for good."

Weekly? Jeanie sank onto the couch. "For good? What do you mean?"

"Oh. I just assumed you knew. . . . Steven and I are getting married."

twelve

"That's w—wonderful. Congratulations." Popcorn rained onto the couch and tumbled to the floor.

"Thank you. It's crazy. Me, Miss Independent, giving up my career for a man. But Lindy was a full-time homemaker, and she set the bar high. She always had supper on the table exactly at six, and she ironed his shirts and even did the yard work. If that's what Steven wants in a wife, that's what he'll get. It's a small price to pay, don't you think?"

Jeanie's mouth parted. Her lips wouldn't cooperate. "Wh—when are you getting married?"

The giggle rattled her eardrum. "We don't have a date set yet—you know how Steven is. . . ."

Evidently I don't have a clue. "Uh-huh."

"But I'd love you to make our cake."

Eyes focused on nothing, Jeanie nodded.

"Jeanie?"

"Oh. . .yes, of course. I'd be. . .honored."

Gretchen made a funny little gasp that Jeanie couldn't decipher. "Jeanie?"

Please, please don't ask if I'm okay with this. "Yes?"

"Are you okay with this?"

Lord, forgive me, I'm about to lie. She sucked in a ragged breath. "Of course! Yes, of course. Congratulations."

"Thank you. I just don't want anything straining our friendship." She gave a tittery laugh. "After all, I'm going to be your daughter's stepmother."

The popcorn bag let out a *whoosh* as Jeanie crushed it into the couch cushion. Lifting it, she crunched it again before firing it at the TV. It dropped to the floor, leaving behind a greasy mark on the screen. Jeanie looked down at the matching stain on the cushion. "Gretchen, my mother just got home." *From taking the trash to the curb.* The statement was irrelevant, but at least it was true. "Congratulations again. Bye."

"Okay, bye. See you on Wednesday."

Not a chance. I'm going to be so sick by Wednesday.

❧

". . .and how would you feel about green and gold for our colors?"

Steven switched the phone to his other hand, rubbed his sore earlobe, and took a glass out of the cupboard. He knew he'd be in trouble if he said "feel" and "color" didn't belong in the same sentence. "I don't think that would go over so well up here. How about blue and orange instead?"

"Steven. . ." Was that a gag on the other end?

He couldn't resist pushing it. "Let's reconsider. If we get married in Dallas we can do blue and silver."

"Oh. . .I get it, silly. We are absolutely not doing football colors."

"That's what people will think." He poured a glass of grape juice. "I know a few Bears fans who'll boycott the wedding if we do green and gold."

"Steven. . ." His name stretched out on an exhale. "There are a lot of shades of green and gold that won't make anyone think of the Green Bay Packers. You'll see. We are talking fall, right? October, maybe?"

"Sure." He opened cupboards, searching for something to sustain him until he could fix a real dinner. Gretchen had called at ten minutes to five. It was now five to six and Burt would be here any minute. On the bright side, she was speeding his weight loss. "I'll have four days during teacher's convention. I can tack on a couple more. I'll talk to the boys and see if that weekend works for them."

"Have you thought about a honeymoon destination?"

A box of Fiddle Faddle tumbled from the cupboard.

Thankfully, the top was closed. He opened the waxy paper inside and poured a pile of caramel-coated popcorn on the counter. *Honeymoon.* The word painted images. . . . Laughing, whispering, sharing secrets. . . "You've ne—" He cleared his throat, coughed. What was wrong with his voice? "You've never been to the Black Hills, have you?"

Silence.

What did I do now? "Or. . .something else. Maybe something. . .resorty. Cancun?"

Gretchen giggled. "That sounds delightful. I actually just ordered you a Hawaiian shirt. I had a feeling you'd be thinking tropical."

Sand, sweat, and a flowered shirt. Steven threw a kernel of popcorn up toward the ceiling fan and caught it in his mouth. "I love those cute little paper umbrellas they put in your orange juice every morning."

"I know. Me, too. I'll get online and book something so we're all set."

But. . . He squelched the doubts with a toss of a glazed pecan.

"And Jeanie's going to make our cake."

The pecan hit his nose, bounced off the Garfield cookie jar, and hit the floor.

"I just talked to her. Not only that, but she's going to Chicago with us."

The Fiddle Faddle box tipped. Hard-shelled popcorn cascaded onto the tile. "You know. . ." His throat muscles contracted, but there was nothing there to swallow. "I really need to change into work clothes. Burt and I are mowing Emma's lawn and trimming her bushes this evening."

"Is Burt ever going to propose to that poor woman?"

"I don't think so. He's got it too good the way things are. He's got his independence and a woman to take to dinner whenever he gets a little lonely. He's happy."

"Well, I'm certainly glad you don't think that way."

"Yeah. Me—" His voice faked out again. He ran to the sink, turned on the faucet, and slurped water out of his hand.

"Are you okay?"

"Yeah, fine. Have a good night. I'll talk to you tomorrow."

"Okay. Bye. Love you." She ended the connection before he had to reply.

❧

Jeanie reread the e-mail from her daughter, plopped her laptop on the grease-stained couch cushion, and stomped into the kitchen. She stared down at the plate of spaghetti on the counter. The reheated supper that had made her stomach growl before the "You've got mail" *ding* now made her stomach twist in knots that wouldn't allow for food. Retracing her steps to the living room, she narrowed her eyes at the computer, wondering if it would cost more to replace the glass on the picture behind the couch or the window over the garage. If she had the money to replace the laptop, it would have sailed into one or the other seconds ago.

> *Hi from the Grand Canyon—*
> *Just got a call from Steven's (still not sure I can ever call him Dad) fiancée. She said you're going to Chicago with her. How are you doing with the news of their engagement? I wish I was there to see for myself that you're okay. As awkward as it is, we are all going to be family soon.*
>
> Love you,
> *A*

Jeanie strode back into the kitchen, pivoted, and walked into the bedroom. She had no idea what she was after when she got there. *We're all going to be family soon.* The mocking voice in her head wouldn't stop. The gall of that woman! Getting Angel involved was nothing short of manipulative. What was Gretchen's angle? Was she hoping to get a free wedding cake out of their "friendship"?

The bedroom mirror reflected a woman with both hands curled in fists and her jaw set in a tight straight line. *This isn't me, Lord. I don't do bitterness. I'm not an angry person. Help me move past this.*

Her walking shoes lay on the floor beside the bed. She kicked out of the Garfield slippers she'd bought on a crazy whim at a 70-percent-off sale. A good, fast walk could do wonders.

She covered the spaghetti and stuck it in the refrigerator. Maybe when her head cleared her stomach would be willing to accept supper.

Seconds into her therapy session, she heard her name shouted from across the street.

"Lucas! Hi!"

Carrying his sport coat over his shoulder, he crossed the quiet street and met her at the corner of Broadway and Meeker. "Trying out for the Olympics, sweet pea?" Deep lines framed his eyes.

"Working off a little steam."

"You? You're the epitome of calm and serenity."

"That was the old me."

Lucas's laugh rumbled across the cobblestones. "Had supper yet?"

She kicked a stone, sending it rolling into the bushes. "I fixed supper. Does that count?"

"Let me treat you to a carnivorous meal at the Log Cabin. Eating like a caveman is good for frustration."

Her eyes closed and she let out another in a long line of sighs. "Supper sounds wonderful, but could we go somewhere else?"

"Old memories?"

She nodded.

"Fried Green Tomatoes?"

"New memories."

"Girl, you can't escape memories in a historic town."

The laugh that bubbled up from some deep-down place surprised her. "Guess I should stop trying."

❧

Staring up at a little stone troll perched on a brick ledge at The Market House Restaurant, Jeanie finally felt her irritation ebb away. She looked across the table. "You're a good listener, Lucas."

"It's part of my job description." He laid his fork on his salad plate and pushed it to the edge of the table. "The more I know about a person, the more chance they're going to love what I design for them." He pulled a pen out of his shirt pocket and lifted his water glass from a cocktail napkin. "Here, I'll design a piece for you—as if I'd only met you tonight, based on what I've just heard."

"No! It'll be ugly. A black dagger piercing a heart or something Goth like that. Design something for the old me."

"Calm and serene?"

"Yes." She leaned forward and watched his pen arc across the napkin.

"A swirl of silver curves embracing a round diamond. . ."

Jeanie groaned.

"I mean sapphire." He looked up at her. "A round, ice-blue sapph—"

"Hi, Jeanie."

Steven stood three feet away. He was with a large man with tattoos on both arms.

Her brain misfired. For a moment she only stared. "Steven. Hello." She gestured across the table. "You know Lucas."

Steven nodded and some kind of silent communication passed between his eyes and Lucas's. "This is Burt Jacobs. Maybe you've met—he's older than most of the buildings around here."

The taller man held out a large, calloused hand, first to Jeanie. "Steven gets *wise* confused with *old* sometimes. I've been in your bakery a time or two."

"You look a bit familiar."

"I'm the 'two chocolate-covered donuts and a bismarck' guy." He shook Lucas's hand. "Don't think we've met."

"We could have. I'm the jeweler across the street from Angel Wings."

"Never had reason to darken the door of a jewelry store."

Lucas smiled at the men. "Why don't you join us for dinner? By the time we get to dessert I'll have a ring designed to match that skull and crossbones." He pointed to Burt's arm and pushed two chairs out with his feet.

Lucas Zemken, you'll pay for this.

Burt sat. "Thank you. I'm not into death symbols anymore, but we'd love to join you for dinner." He looked up at Steven with what could only be labeled triumph. "Take a load off, Vandenburg."

Steven seemed beyond reluctant as he took the only empty chair, to her right.

Act normal. She pushed aside her half-eaten salad. *We're all going to be family soon.* The unwelcome echo in her head caused her fingers to tangle on her fork. Metal clanged against glass, displacing a piece of lettuce and a grape tomato. "We've. . .already ordered."

"No problem." Burt waved down the waiter. "We'll have whatever they're having. Unless it's more rabbit food." He pointed at the tomato rolling toward him.

The waiter scribbled on his pad. "Two half-pound tavern burgers with fries. How would you like them prepared?"

"Just past the moo for me, medium for this guy."

"I'll get that right in. What can I bring you to drink while. . ."

The man's voice faded in the distance as Jeanie aimed her glare at the vines spilling over the stone wall. . .to keep from burning Lucas with it.

". . .since I became a Christian. Maybe you could design me one of those Celtic crosses. My family's from Wales—"

"Seriously? My father grew up in. . ."

Again, the sounds grew faint. Steven was looking at her. She put on her best smile. "Congratulations on your engagement."

"Thank you." He played with a button on his polo shirt. "Did Gretchen give you details on the pizza sale?"

This was not good. All that work to come up with a plausible excuse—she had to cook for her mother's Red Hat Society meeting that weekend—and Gretchen hadn't even told him about the message she'd left. "I. . .as it turns out, I won't be able to make it after all. I have to. . .cater. . . lunch for. . .a local organization next Saturday." *The local organization consisting of my mother and five of her friends.*

"Oh." Like a polygraph, his expression told her she hadn't pulled it off. But he seemed relieved.

"You have plenty of help, don't you?" The question came from her heart, not her brain, and slipped out her mouth before she had time to override it.

A subtle shift transformed Steven's expression. "To be honest, we really don't. If you change your mind, I'd really appreciate it."

The blue gaze that had milked more volunteer hours out of Jeanie Cholewinski than any high school student had ever sacrificed for the literary digest was working its dangerous wonder once again. "Well. . ."

Their waiter approached, bringing burgers. . .and common sense. She suddenly knew what the subtle change had been: hope. And not because he needed more hands making pizza. Jeanie shook her head, not enough for Steven to see, but enough to clear it momentarily. If for no other reason, she had to say no for Gretchen's sake.

Lucas thanked the waiter. "Could we have a couple of extra plates? We'll share ours until theirs is ready."

Burt held up his hand. "I'll wait. Nobody wants to share mine."

Steven looked at Jeanie's plate. "Still medium-rare with

tomato, lettuce, and mayo?"

Dumbly, she nodded. They'd never once eaten out together. "How could you remember that?"

"I remember ev—" He stopped and stared, first at Burt, then at Lucas. His face colored. The two men were silent and gawking.

With identically smug smiles on their Welsh faces.

❧

As Jeanie walked in the kitchen door, the *ding* sounded from her computer. She put her phone on the table, walked to the bedroom door, then turned around. Maybe this time it wasn't an e-mail from her daughter reminding her they'd all be family soon. Maybe it was from someone in her Bible study group. . .something newsy or encouraging that would get her mind off how easy the evening had been. Too easy, after the first few awkward moments. Too much finishing each other's sentences, and way, way too much familiarity from a man who was engaged to be married in three months.

She walked back to the couch and sat down.

Angel. Again. The subject line read *one more thing.*

Just thought of something. Why don't you bring Taylor to Chicago with you? That would save Wade's parents a trip. Maybe she'd even like to help with the pizza sale. Wouldn't her jabbering make a great buffer?

Buffer. Would a buffer be enough when what she really needed was a drawbridge, a mote, and an iron shield?

But she had to learn to do this, to be around Steven and not just act okay, but actually *be* okay. With one last sigh for the day, she pulled her phone out of her pocket and went to the text message screen. She found Taylor's number in her Contacts list.

TELL YOUR PARENTS I'LL GIVE YOU A RIDE HOME ON FRIDAY. That would buffer one day.

HAVE PLANS FOR SATURDAY? WANT TO HELP WITH A PIZZA SALE IN THE CITY?

She pushed SEND, closed the phone, then opened it again.

YOU CAN RIDE BACK HERE WITH ME—AND STEVEN—ON SUNDAY.

thirteen

"That was so thoughtful of you to make that scrapbook for Steven." Gretchen snapped a picture as Jeanie stuck a spoon in a Ball jar of homemade raspberry filling.

Ladling the filling into a sieve to strain out the seeds, Jeanie shrugged. "I thought it would help him"—*Help him what? See everything he'd missed?* She spread a circle of filling onto the last cake layer—"get to know her more."

"I looked at the book last night. Angel is a beautiful young woman. Did something happen to her baby pictures or was it that you just couldn't afford them?"

Jeanie picked up another cake layer. "It was. . .a difficult time." *But I took pictures. So many pictures. . .*

Gretchen moved her reflective umbrella to the other side of the cake and took another shot. The last of the natural light through the high windows was quickly fading. "I can identify with some of what you went through."

I don't think that's possible. "How is that?"

"My husband was in the Navy. He was killed in 1987 when his ship was struck by Iraqi missiles in the Persian Gulf. I was pregnant at the time."

The cake layer tipped precariously. Jeanie righted it and set it firmly in place. "I didn't realize. . .you have a child?"

Short dark hair brushed against large pearl earrings. "He was stillborn. The doctors thought the stress of my husband's death. . ." Soft smile lines appeared. "It wasn't meant to be. But I can understand the difficulty of going through a pregnancy alone."

Heaviness pushed against Jeanie's chest. "I'm so sorry, Gretchen."

"Thank you. That was a long time ago. And God uses everything for good, doesn't He? Like it says in second Corinthians, He gives us opportunities to comfort others in the way we have been comforted."

Steven. Gretchen had a bond with him she could never fully understand. "I'm sure Steven was very grateful to have you there when he lost his wife."

"We held each other up." Gretchen looked down and fiddled with the lens on her camera. "He and Lindy were there for me when Andrew died."

"How long have you known each other?"

"Lindy and I became friends at Texas State. I remember when she first started talking about this tall blond guy she met." The camera flashed again. "They were so happy together. But I wonder, now that I've met you. . ." She shook her head and removed the lens.

"Wonder what?"

"Lindy always said she could never have all of him."

Jeanie swallowed hard, picked up a new jar of raspberry filling, and set it down again. "What did she mean by that?"

"She knew he'd left a little part of himself somewhere in his past. I don't think he ever told her about you."

Picking up the jar again, Jeanie nodded. "I'm sure he was ashamed of our decisions and just wanted to forget."

Gretchen's lips pressed together. Small puckers formed at the corners of her mouth. "I don't—"

A knock at the front door rescued Jeanie from the end of Gretchen's statement. "Excuse me." Wiping her hands, she walked through the dimly lit shop and waved through the window at Lucas. She unlocked the door and opened it wide. "Come in."

"Can I watch the photo shoot?"

"Absolutely." *Thank you, thank you.* She led him into the back and introduced the jeweler to the photographer.

Lucas took Gretchen's hand in both of his. "So you're the

woman stealing my chance at fame."

"Oh, I—"

Lucas laughed and pumped her hand. "Just kidding. I'm a very amateur amateur and Jeanie deserves the best." He let go of her hand and pointed to the camera on the table next to the cake. "Nikon F6. Nice." He picked it up, squinting as if he were looking at a diamond. "I've wanted a micro lens like this for years. I want to take my own pictures for my Web site. Do you like it?"

"Love it. It would be perfect for jewelry. . .if you have the right lighting." Gretchen pulled another lens out of her bag and handed it to him. "I'd be more than happy to take pictures for you."

"Well, next time you're up here, let me know. I'll see if I can afford you."

A laugh and a bounce of curls on pearls accompanied Gretchen's emphatic head shake. "No charge for a friend of Jeanie's. We're almost done here for tonight. I'd be happy to bring my equipment over when we finish."

"Tonight? Well. . .sure. I'd better go get things ready then." Lucas set down the lenses and took two steps toward the door to the shop. "But I will pay you somehow. Everyone needs the services of a jeweler from time to time."

Gretchen grinned. "Actually, I am in need of just such service." She waved. "We'll talk." She turned back to Jeanie, a wistful smile tilting her mouth. "I was going to say that I agree with Lindy." She turned and snapped a lens into its case.

&

"You were up mighty early this morning." Her mother pulled a new box of bakery tissue out of the closet. "I heard you leave at three. Someone on your mind?"

"Some*thing*. Things." Jeanie set a fondant ribbon on the cake and stretched her neck. A headache was inevitable. "We're leaving at one. I have to have this done by ten so Gretchen can do the final shoot and then run home and shower and pack and—"

The door buzzer sounded. Her mother left to wait on the customer. Jeanie rested her hands on the table and closed her eyes. *Lord, calm me.* Anxiety over the next two days and stress from the past two had rubbed her nerves raw. Gretchen had been helpful, kind, and so transparent. The proofs she'd developed were stunning, and Jeanie was more grateful than she could put into words. But the constant chatter had worn her patience thinner than phyllo dough. *Help me to be gracious to her. . .and cautious with Steven. Let me be—*

"Jeanie." Her mother's voice reached the room before she did. "There's a man asking for you." Tiny creases rutted her mother's forehead. She turned around and walked back.

Jeanie's pulse skipped, then raced. *Damon.* By the look on her mother's face it had to be. She couldn't send her mother away like she had Taylor. What should she do if Damon called her Misty? Laugh? Pretend the man was crazy? Pretend. . . Her legs trembled from fear and exhaustion. She'd spent twenty-five years pretending three years of her life had never happened.

The truth will set you free.

At what cost?

Weighted legs carried her to the front where Damon stood with a white bag in his hand and two paper cups with lids.

Jeanie stepped to her mother's left. "What do you want?" She kept her tone flat, devoid of emotion.

Damon flashed false teeth in a smile that bowed his mustache and sent icy fingers down her back. "I was just chatting with your mom about this quaint little town and I got to thinking about that opportunity I told you about. It occurred to me that we could run a satellite business right here in Galena—lots of traffic running through here during tourist season. You could be our talent scout, so to speak." His laugh brought acid to her throat. Black, beady eyes chilled her. "Have you told your mom about the job I offered you?"

Her hand rose, closed over the wall phone. Her eyes narrowed, never leaving the evil face.

Damon lifted the bakery bag. "Sorry, *Jeanie*. Got to run. I'll talk to you. . .soon."

The door buzzed as the man in black walked out to the bleached blond waiting in his convertible.

Her mother grabbed her arm. "Who was that? How do you know him?"

Jeanie's head felt light. She couldn't think straight. "He. . .used to work with me. . .in California." *And Reno.* "He's thinking of starting a. . .business."

"What kind of business? There's something frightening about him. I don't think you should get involved with—"

"I have no intention of working with that man." She took a shuddering breath and gave a pretend smile. "I need. . .to finish."

On legs that felt like lead, she walked to the back.

❧

A shrill scream burst from the living room. Jeanie's pulse skipped. Her mother's favorite mug banged against the side of the suds-filled sink. She turned around. "Taylor? What happened?"

"I wish my mother would quit going all multiball on me!" Wearing tan shorts and a white T-shirt, Taylor appeared in the kitchen doorway, cell phone in hand. Sunny trailed close behind. "She isn't consistent on anything. First she's okay with me living here, then she thinks it would be better if I came home for good, then she says I should be home for the summer and maybe I can go to school here again in the fall. . . she's schizo."

"You just gave me a heart attack because your mother wants you home?" Jeanie made a noose with her thumbs and index fingers. "I oughta. . ."

"Hey, cool it. You're wound really tight today."

"I'm just a little. . .stressed." Her attempt at a laugh missed.

She walked over and tugged on a pigtail as she opened the closet and took out a broom. "Did you ever stop to think that you might be the cause of your mother being a schizo? Maybe she's a little nuts because she's having trouble keeping up with you. Look at you. . . . When we first met you, your hair was two different colors and everything was pierced. A few months later and you're all earthy and back-to-nature girl. . . . You make *my* head spin."

"I'm working on myself. My changes are good. Hers aren't. We used to get along." Taylor stretched her arms over her head and touched the frame over the doorway. "Now it's just always. . . ugly. Maybe I should do her a big favor and just disappear."

The broom stopped mid-sweep. "You don't mean that."

Taylor lowered her arms and shrugged. "Did you and your mother ever fight?"

A laugh sounded from above the kitchen. "Still do!" echoed through the old iron grate.

"And mothers never stop sticking their noses in your business!" Jeanie tapped the ceiling with the end of the broom.

Taylor's nose wrinkled. "You guys have such a cool relationship. I could never goof around with my mom like that."

This time, the laugh was a duet between Jeanie and the voice through the vent. "Do you have any idea how 'cool' our relationship was when I was your age?"

"When you were sneaking out to see Mr. Vandenburg? Shouldn't he be here by now?"

"Any minute. Are you all ready?"

"Yeah. Can't we take Sunny?" Taylor kneeled down and wrapped her arms around the dog.

"Only if he can sit on your lap for three hours."

"Cool!"

"I was kidding."

"So did Mr. Vandenburg have hair like MacGyver?"

"No, he had a neon pink Mohawk and he wore leather pants with chains."

"For real?"

"No." Jeanie ignored the tongue sticking out at her as she swept under the table. "He was a student teacher. He dressed very respectably." *Except for the jeans and sleeveless Ocean Pacific shirts he wore after school. . .after dark. . .*

"I heard a car door. I don't have to sit in back with Gretchen, do I?"

"Of course not, she'll sit in front with Steven. She's his fiancée." *Keep saying it, maybe it'll seem real.*

"Good. That lady's loony. I mean, she's nice, but she's loony. I was so glad when she left this morning. She talks like nonstop. My head was spinning."

Oh, how I know the feeling. "She means well. Her metabolism's just set at a higher notch than some of—"

The screen door squeaked open. "Sorry we're late." Gretchen stepped in wearing white walking shorts and a yellow blouse trimmed in rhinestones. "We were looking at rings. Practically had to drag that man into the jewelry store. Men! Lucas was so accommodating. I'd love to just sit and watch him sometime. He asked so many questions. I think he should teach classes to men, don't you? Most men don't know how to ask the kind of questions that make a woman think he's genuinely interested. Taylor"—Gretchen pointed at her—"look for a man who asks questions. Not that you should be looking yet, but when you're older. Maybe you should look for a jeweler! I know more about diamonds now than I ever dreamed of. I'm leaning toward a princess cut. Something different, you know. Everybody ready?"

Jeanie shot a warning at Taylor as the girl's eyes rolled toward the ceiling, down to the left, and back to the ceiling.

As ready as we'll ever be.

❧

"Have these kids had any kitchen experience?" Jeanie directed the question to the middle of the front seat between Steven and Gretchen.

"Some." Steven looked at her in the rearview mirror. Did he have to do that? "They're all at least sixteen, and the shelter is teaching them basic job skills for working in restaurants, hotels, school kitchens, things like that. They're all kids who've expressed an interest in that kind of work, so they should be cooperative and teachable. But they come from dysfunctional backgrounds. You may find some who won't say a word and some who won't shut up."

Taylor's index finger jabbed into Jeanie's forearm, then pointed toward Gretchen.

"Shush," Jeanie breathed.

Gretchen turned and looked over her seat. "They make me uncomfortable. I got the feeling last year that they didn't trust us. They know we've never experienced anything close to the kind of life they have."

If only that were true. "I went on a couple of inner-city ministry trips to Mexico with our church years ago. I've never done anything like that in the States, but I think kids must be kind of the same all over."

"Mexico City?" Steven's eyes rose to the rearview mirror.

"Yes."

Gretchen reached back and touched Jeanie's knee. "*Ciudad de México.* Isn't it an amazing place? The National Palace, Morelia Cathedral, Teotihuacán—The City of the Gods. And the food. . .what was your favorite?—

"Well, actually. . ."

"She was there on a mission trip," Steven said. "She probably didn't get much chance to sightsee or taste the cuisine."

"Oh. . .I suppose that's true." Gretchen pulled her arm back and turned around.

Taylor's hand slid over her mouth. "Awkward," she whispered.

Jeanie looked down at her watch. Two hours and thirty minutes left.

Lord, help.

fourteen

"I love squishing it with my hands." A'isha, an eighteen-year-old who was seven months pregnant, held up a ball of dough in her latex-gloved hand.

"It's called kneading," Gretchen corrected.

"Whatever. I *knead* to squish this stuff!" A'isha took a clumsy bow when her friends standing around the table laughed. A boy with black dreadlocks stuffed into a white hairnet threw his dough to a gangly kid with pants in danger of ending up around his ankles. Three more dough balls took flight.

Jeanie glanced at the next table. Steven's group worked like a well-trained assembly line, spreading pizza sauce and sprinkling cheese. Her thumb and fingers went to her mouth and a commotion-freezing whistle split the air. She had their attention. Shaping her hands into a catcher's mitt, she called across the table, "Throw it to me, A'isha."

The ball flew. She caught it and held it up. "Okay, we got rules here. No throwing dough unless you can *throw* dough. Everybody watching?" She dumped a cup of flour on the table, smoothed it out, and set the dough on it. Quick motions pressed it down and formed an edge. With a rolling pin, she flattened it and shaped a new edge. Picking it up, she stretched it over upturned fingers, her hands vibrating.

"You can't really do what I think you're gonna do!" Blue eyes wide, a skinny girl in a hot pink shirt gaped.

"Everybody watching?"

Taylor covered her face with her arms.

The thin, wiggly sheet flew into the air. The dough circle spun three feet above her head and landed over the backs of her hands. The table exploded in applause and whistles.

"Show me!" "Do it again!" "I wanna do that!"

"Me, too!" This was not the voice of a teenager. Steven stood just inches from her left elbow.

Jeanie took a step back. "O. . .kay. Turn your hands over and alternate them with mine."

His hands slid into place under the dough, touching hers. Blue eyes glimmered. "Make me look good, Dreamy."

This was not the time for vibrating hands. But she couldn't control it. "Twist one arm to the outside, just a little, like this. The other arm pulls back slightly. Feel it?"

"Mm-hmm." Dimples indented his cheeks and warmed hers.

"Then throw up your hands. . .and stop. The fast stop is what tosses it in the air. Up and stop, and catch it with the backs of your hands. Got it?"

"I think so."

She dipped her hands from under the dough. Steven's arms flew up and halted. The dough sailed off his hands, across the table. . .and hit the little blond girl squarely in the face.

Cheers filled the kitchen. Jeanie doubled over laughing and Steven bent with her. His arm slid around her shoulders, pulling her into a quick hug.

She knew she should push him away, but for the moment she couldn't remember why.

❧

Taylor slipped two unbaked pizzas into the commercial freezer and took two more pans from Nevin, a basketball player–sized boy who seemed to be taking a liking to her. Taylor smiled at him, and Jeanie's fingers tightened around the package of cheese she was sealing. She'd have to keep an eye on those two.

Nevin pushed an empty roller cart toward the wall and Taylor nudged Jeanie. "So why does he call you Dreamy?"

Jeanie glanced across the room where Steven and Gretchen were washing dishes with a group of kids. At that moment, Steven turned around and smiled. Just the way he used to back when he'd told her he had radar that detected her every move in class. " 'I Dream of Jeannie' kind of got shortened."

Taylor batted starry eyes. "That's so romantic."

"That's so corny. Get your head on straight, kid." She nodded toward Nevin.

Taylor shrugged off the warning. "It's romantic and you know it. That man's still crazy nuts about you and his woman's figuring it out."

"Hush. What do you mean?"

"Didn't you see her when we were making pizzas? She was eyeing you two up one side and down the other. Didn't you see her walk out?"

"No. Was she. . .mad?"

"More sad, I think."

"I have to talk to her."

Taylor's nose crinkled. "Why? Won't change the truth."

Nevin handed two more pizza trays to Taylor. "We're done. Let's get a soda."

"Okay." Taylor looked up, and up, until her eyes locked on his. *Just stay in plain view.* Jeanie tried to catch the girl's attention for another warning glance, but to no avail. She watched them grab sodas from an ice-filled tub and sit on the floor, their backs to an open shelf, their feet against the wall. *I'm watching you.* She picked up four unused bags of cheese and hugged them to her chest, wrapping her arms around them. As she opened the door of the walk-in cooler with full arms, she knocked a massive padlock from its shelf. It skittered like a hockey puck into the cooler. She shelved the bags, and as she got down on all fours to retrieve the lock, her own radar picked up Steven's scent. Not cologne, not deodorant, but the scent of *him.* She steadied her breathing and stood up.

"We need to talk."

Her arms folded against the chill. "About what?"

"I can't do this, Jeanie. I can't. . .be around you. What happened earlier. . .hugging you. . .it's too automatic, too easy to fall back into what we used to be. I can't do this."

I can't either. But with Gretchen within earshot, this wasn't the time to talk. "We're adults, Steven. We can do this. Someday we're going to have grandkids, and we'll both be there for birthdays and dedications. We have to be able to be in the same room with each other. We need to move on. I'm going to Paris to finally start living my life." The tear that slid down her cheek startled her. "You're getting married, starting a whole new—"

His hand slammed against a metal shelf. "I'm getting married because you won't admit you're still in love with me."

She froze. Like a key with just the right notches, tumblers turned, unlocking the truth. *Lord. . .* She stared into penetrating blue eyes. *It's time.* Even if Gretchen was around the corner. She closed her eyes. "Steven. . ."

"I can't do this friends thing, Jeanie. I don't want to go to Angel's house and see you there. I don't want to do holidays together like some big happy family. I don't want to be around you. Do you understand?"

Muffled laughter from the kitchen made the moment surreal. Steven stared, as if memorizing every inch of her face in the light of the single bulb hanging above them. Slowly, he shook his head.

"Steven. I have to tell—"

He held up his hand. "Don't say anything." He turned and walked out, his steps echoing across the tile.

"Steven! Wait!" She followed him into the kitchen. "Let me—"

Gretchen walked out between two rows of shelves. Her hand reached out and slid into his and they walked together up the stairs.

❧

"Are we ever gonna get done with this?" Tess, Steven's dough target, threw an empty pizza sauce can in the trash. "I'm too tired to breathe and we gotta come back and work all day tomorrow sellin' this stuff."

"Take off. I'll finish this." Jeanie formed her lips into a smile. "See you in the morning, Tess." *If I'm here.*

The girl waved and Jeanie picked up a plastic tub of olive oil. Thoughts ricocheted as she walked toward the shelves. She had to decide, once and for all—walk away from Steven, protect her pride and Gretchen's happiness, and never look back, or force Steven to listen as she poured out every last little detail and leave the decision to him.

Walking between two ceiling-high open shelves, she found the marked spot. As she slid the tub of oil into place, she heard Taylor's laugh. She leaned toward the voices.

". . .serious. You got the perfect look—tall and thin with great skin and beautiful features. The right hair and makeup and you'll be a goddess. You'll be making a hundred grand by Christmas, no lie. And think what this could lead to. Clothes, cars, jewelry, and all you gotta do is smile and pose and sometimes be somebody's arm candy. Rich guys pay big just to have some gorgeous model to show off at a party."

Jeanie clamped both hands on the shelf. She had to hear more before she acted. No, she had to do more than hear. She opened her phone, dialed her home number, and set it on a salt box on a low shelf. At that moment, Steven walked past the end of the shelf. In two quick steps, she grabbed his shirtsleeve and put her fingers to his lips. Cupping her hand around his ear, she pointed and whispered, "Listen."

". . .sixteen. My parents wouldn't allow it. Maybe after high sch—"

"You just said you're sick of your mom freaking out on you and changing her mind all the time. You gonna do what your parents say forever? Think about all that jewelry and stuff. Think about how proud your parents will be when you send 'em megachecks. There might not be an opening in two years and besides, you got the look now. It'll change when you. . .you know, mature. Right now you got what my boss is looking for."

"I don't know. . ." A sigh was followed by a tapping sound, like fingernails on tile.

"Gimme a week, okay? Come with me and give it a try. See if you don't love bein' a rich girl."

Jeanie's stomach muscles spasmed. She put both hands over her mouth.

"I came here with Jeanie. What do I say to her?"

"Nothin'. She'll figure you're with me. You know, like you and me got a thing for each other. . .which we do, right?"

The shelves towering over her seemed to tilt. The space between them grew narrower. *Hide. Find a place where he can't find us.* Her hands slid to her eyes, to stop the black spots. Steven stepped closer. He pulled her hands away from her face, his eyes searching hers. She looked down, found his phone clipped to his belt, and pulled it off. She turned off the sound and dialed 911, then set his phone beside hers. Pointing to the end of the shelves, she motioned for him to go around one end while she went the other way. "Act casual," she whispered against his ear.

She waited until she heard him say, "Hi, guys." Nice and calm. Did he have the slightest clue what was happening?

She squeezed between the wall and the end of the shelf. "I heard you offering Taylor a job, Nevin."

The boy squirmed, drew his long legs up to his chest. "Yeah. I think she'd be a great model. . .when she grows up."

"But you said—"

He shot Taylor a silencing look.

Jeanie smiled. Nice and casual. "Modeling job. . . Your boss sends you out on the street looking for pretty young girls, huh?" She raised her voice, hoping she'd be heard on the other end of the phone on the shelf.

The boy's eyes darted toward the door leading up to the street.

Jeanie crossed her arms, leaned down close, raking him with her eyes. "It's a prostitution ring, isn't it, Nevin? Recruitin' right here out of the kitchen at the Twenty-Fourth Street Mission. Clever."

❧

Steven's pulse hammered in his ears. He stared at the woman he once knew, interrogating a man a foot taller than her like a seasoned cop.

"Don't get all fidgety. I'm not ratting on you, Nevin." She laughed, leaned against the wall, and folded her arms. "Your name isn't Nevin, is it?"

The boy didn't move.

"Yeah, I didn't think so. I used to go by Misty. Seems we're in the same line of work."

What?

"What?" Taylor's eyes popped wide.

Jeanie flung her braid over her shoulder. "Well, I'm retired, but I used to do just what you're doing. They call you a recruiter?"

Nevin shook his head. "I'm a scout."

Taylor gasped. Steven crouched down and pulled her to him, never taking his eyes off Jeanie. She was amazing, playing the part as realistically as any Hollywood actress.

"They gave you some pretty good training. You're smooth. Me, I had to learn on the job." Her eyes turned to steel. Fingernails pressed into her arm. "So what got you into this line of work, Nevin? Hey, what's your real name? You know mine."

"Craig." His voice was barely audible.

"Craig. Now that fits you. Sounds like a basketball player. So what was it got you into this?"

"My brother. He's making good money."

"I bet he is. What's your brother's name?"

"Wil. . ." He stopped, looked from Jeanie to Steven. "I gotta get out of here." He jumped to his feet.

Steven stood, pulling Taylor with him. He was at eye-level to the boy's Adam's apple, but he put his hand on his arm. It was his turn to take part in Jeanie's charade to stall him. "We're kind of like Taylor's guardians right now, Craig. I imagine we could get a pretty kickback if we let her work for you. What guarantee do we have that she won't get hurt?" Taylor tried to wrench away, but he held her tight. *Play along, kid.*

"I don't. . .I don't know. I just find 'em. It's not my business what happens after that."

Jeanie took a step toward him. "Really? They should give you a promotion, Craig. When I was in the business I wasn't just a recruiter, I was a chauffeur."

Transfixed by her skill, Steven almost smiled. The woman was good.

"Got to transport the girls, see them settled into a nice, cushy mansion. Had my own room there, too. Gold faucets. You got gold faucets, *Nevin?*"

"No. *No.*" He pulled his arm from Steven. Jeanie grabbed his elbow. The boy raised his arm and swung, slamming Jeanie into a metal grate covering a window, and took off at a run.

Another set of footsteps echoed in the hallway, then more. "Police! Stop!"

Steven held his breath, waiting for a gunshot, but silence followed. He dropped to his knees and wrapped his arms around Jeanie. "Taylor, reach through there and grab my phone." As she did, he pressed Jeanie's head to his chest. "Are you okay?"

She nodded against his shirt and wrapped her arms around him.

"Everything I said before, forget it," he whispered against her hair. "I can't *not* be around you."

fifteen

She hadn't been held like this in so long. Again, the voice that said she shouldn't be allowing this clamored too distantly to obey. All that mattered was the moment. Steven's voice reverberating in his chest as he spoke to the dispatcher. . .the smell of him, musky, earthy. . .muscles forming ridges on his forearms. . .his fingertips brushing a rhythm on her shoulder.

If, after all he'd just heard, he could still hold her like he never wanted to let her go, maybe she'd been wrong. Maybe she didn't need to keep her guard up. Maybe, for the first time in thirty years, she could stop pretending. Her ugly secret was exposed. . .to the one person who had the most right to judge her. . .and he hadn't pushed her away.

Her hip throbbed, her elbow stung. Her leg tingled from the awkward position. Yet she felt more at peace than she had in years. As if she could finally take a full breath. She closed her eyes, letting the stroke of his fingertips push away the pain, the fear, and anger that had coursed through her veins moments earlier. She pressed her cheek into his shirt and let out the breath, long and slow.

She was safe.

Steven closed his phone. His left arm completed her circle of safety. "Paramedics are on their way."

She nodded. Words might break the spell.

"You were amazing," he whispered.

"Yeah. That was wild." Taylor's cold hand slid over hers. "Was all that stuff really true?"

"Of course it wasn't!" Steven's laugh echoed beneath his ribs.

Her diaphragm locked, lungs half full. Her chest shook

with the thudding of her heart. Sparks of silver light pricked her eyes. Numb, as if she were watching someone else's body stiffen, she pulled back, looked up into cobalt eyes. "It. . .it is true. All of it." She moved away, opening the circle.

An airy whistle blew through Taylor's pursed lips.

Steven's hands tightened on her arms. "I don't. . .understand."

Could she possibly make him see? Make him feel the fear? Taste the hopelessness? A siren wailed. She lifted her hand, laid it against his cheek. "I couldn't—"

Taylor jabbed her leg.

Eyes red, fingers covering her mouth, Gretchen stood at the end of the shelf. "Are you all right?"

As if touching live coals, Jeanie's hand drew back. Steven dropped his hands to his thighs. "We're fine. Taylor was in trouble and we—"

"Good. Good." Gretchen nodded, eyes now glassy, and ran out of the kitchen.

⁂

Jeanie woke on Saturday morning surrounded by purple pillows. Angel's apartment. Angel's *old* apartment. She closed her eyes again as a strange heaviness pulled her into the mattress. Why was she so tired? She turned toward the clock and gasped. Hot needles shot from elbow to shoulder.

Stitches. The ER. They'd given her a sleeping pill.

Nevin. As of midnight, they hadn't caught him. He'd be far from the city by now.

The apartment was quiet. Pug had told her to sleep as late as she could. She'd offered to take Taylor to the pizza sale.

The pizza sale! She should be there. She opened one eye, searching for the clock. Almost nine. The sale had started. But she was going home today, taking a bus, wasn't she? Wasn't that what she'd decided? Her thoughts slowed. No, she was going to talk to Steven. Her eyes closed; once again she was circled in his arms. So warm, so safe. . .

He knew! Her eyes shot open. Steven knew. He'd disappeared

when the paramedics arrived. She had to explain. No matter what—even if he refused to ever look at her again—he had to know she hadn't chosen that life, had to know she'd tried to escape, tried to get back. . .to him.

But would he even listen?

Ignoring the pain that taunted her whole right side, she pulled on her clothes and called a cab.

❧

The sidewalk in front of the Twenty-Fourth Street Mission swarmed with people carrying pizza boxes or shouting orders at the harried teens behind the table.

"Jeanie!" A'isha waved her toward the cash register table. "Hey, come here a sec."

Her hopes of quietly talking to Steven evaporated. "How's it going A'isha?"

"Fine, but. . ." The girl shifted her pregnant weight from one foot to the other. "Could you take over for a minute? Everybody's busy and I gotta. . .you know."

"Sure." Jeanie laughed and shooed her on her way as a dark-skinned woman with graying hair held up two frozen pizzas and a twenty. Jeanie shoved aside A'isha's pile of soda cans and candy wrappers, uncovering the price list. "That'll be eighteen dollars." Jeanie entered the amount and reached in the drawer for two singles.

"Keep the change." The woman waved at the money Jeanie held out to her. "I lived here once. Wish I could do more."

As she waited on three more customers, a man stood at the edge of the crowd watching her. A Cubs hat sat low over mirrored sunglasses. He wore a long navy tank top over shiny white shorts that ended mid-calf. To a person without any street sense, the man would just blend with the crowd.

To a person who'd spent three years of her life watching her back, a stationary man in a milling crowd triggered alarms. The man moved into line, the only person empty-handed. His head turned with her every move, his mirrored eyes trained on her. *Hurry, A'isha.*

Two people stood between her and the man. Who was he? Nevin's boss? His brother? What did he want with her? It was too late to stop her from talking. She'd already given a statement. So had Taylor. Taylor. . .where was she? She whirled around, but couldn't spot her. . .or Steven. She counted out change with trembling hands. *Run.* She fought against instinct. She wouldn't leave the money unguarded. The man wouldn't do anything in public. *Where's Taylor?* Something nudged her arm. She jumped.

"I'm back." A'isha rubbed the sides of her belly. "Hey, that was wild about Nevin, huh? Were you really. . ."

The man moved to the head of the line. A'isha's voice faded in the thick air. *Run.*

This time she did. Through the maze of portable freezers and darting kids, over the roadblock that fenced out customers, up the steps, into the cool shadow of the crumbling brick building.

The door stood open. She flew in, down the steps, into the kitchen. "Taylor!" Where was she? "Taylor!"

Tess ran out from between the shelves. "What's wrong?" Her pale faced grew instantly paler.

"Where's Taylor?"

"She went to the store with that lady. . .Gretchen."

"Thank God."

"Why? What's. . ."

Footsteps slapped the stairs. Jeanie's gaze swept the room. *Hide. Find a place.* The cooler. She ran to it, heaved the door open, and darted in. Grabbing the inside handle with both hands, she braced her feet. On the other side of the door, someone yelled. A man's voice. The handle moved. She strained against it. It wrenched out of her hands. She opened her mouth to scream.

Steven stood in the open doorway.

Her gasp froze in her throat and air rushed from her lungs.

He took a step toward her. "What hap—"

The door slammed behind him. Something clanged against it. He turned and pushed against the handle.

It wouldn't budge.

≈

"No signal." Steven stuck his phone back on his belt and pounded on the door.

As he yelled and pounded, Jeanie turned in a slow circle, hunting for anything to cover her bare arms.

"We're trapped!" Steven's voice strained on the second word.

A dim memory floated through the chill air. She'd snuck out after midnight. They'd met in a field. It started to rain, and she'd pulled him into an old rusty horse trailer. But he wouldn't let her close the door.

Steven was claustrophobic.

Maybe it was the residual effects of the sleeping pills, or maybe it was the layers of irony—that she, who felt snug and secure in small, dark places, was locked in a cooler with a man who was terrified of them. Whatever the reason, Jeanie began to laugh. So hard she had to grip the metal shelves on either side of her.

Steven turned and gaped at her. "Are you out of your mind?"

"Maybe," she gasped. "Probably. I'm s—sorry."

His back pushed against the door, his finger ran under the collar of his polo shirt. His face flushed and his chest shuddered. If she didn't distract him, she'd be locked in a cooler with a man in a full-blown panic attack. The vision sent the muscles on her sides into spasms again. She spun around. A plastic milk crate full of apples sat in the far corner. She dumped it, sending apples rolling across the floor like pool balls. "Sit down."

He complied. She turned around again. Another crate sat on a low shelf, this one filled with cottage cheese containers.

As she emptied the crate, she said, "Well, at least we won't go hungry. Are you hungry?" She overturned the empty crate and stood on it, eyeing the top shelves. "If I ran a shelter with a ton of kids around, I'd hide the good stuff up high, wouldn't you? Ah! Chocolate!" She reached between two boxes and pulled out a basket teaming with candy bars. She jumped down and sat on the crate with the basket on her knees. "Three Musketeers? No, wait, do you still like Snickers?" Still digging through the basket, she held it out.

He didn't take it. She looked up. His eyes were closed; his head shook. The tip of his tongue was held firmly with his teeth. She waited. His eyes finally opened. A faint smile took the fear from his eyes. "I'd forgotten just how crazy you made me," he whispered. A drawn-out sigh lowered his shoulders. "You always knew how to make me smile."

But this isn't me. I haven't felt silly like this since. . .you. "Steven. . ." She set the basket on the floor. "I need to explain about yesterday."

"One crisis at a time. First explain about today. Was that guy following you?" He described the man with the mirrored glasses.

"Yes. I'm guessing he's Nevin's brother."

"Then it's no accident we're locked in."

She shook her head. "There's a padlock." An involuntary shiver shook her.

"You're freezing." He stood up, walked to the back, and held up two huge flour sack towels that had been covering pans of bread dough. Next he found two mesh bags of oranges. Pulling out a jackknife, he opened the ends and dumped the oranges on the floor. "Hold out your arms." He worked for several minutes, fashioning towel-lined sleeves. "Should help a little. They'll find us soon."

"Thank you." She folded her red mesh-covered arms across her middle. "You're very resourceful."

"It's nothing compared to what you pulled off yesterday."

His eyes didn't reflect the touch of humor in his voice. "You've got a captive audience, might as well put the time to good use and talk. I could say it's none of my business, but I just can't quite bring myself to say that. How old was Angel at the time you had that. . .job?"

She turned away from the interrogating eyes, willing the door to open. "I was pregnant when I started."

A ring of white outlined Steven's lips.

"I'd been at Aunt Freda's for two weeks when I found out I was pregnant. I knew I had to get out of there before she found out. I couldn't take a chance on her telling my mother. I told a waitress at this coffee shop that I needed a job. She introduced me to a guy who was looking for someone to care for his handicapped mother. His name was Val. He said he'd pay for my food, clothes, give me a room of my own."

Steven's fingers curled in toward his palms.

"The job was exactly like he said. He took me to a very classy-looking building in Reno. I had a beautiful room, an unbelievable paycheck, and a charge card for anything I needed. All I had to do was clean his mother's apartment and fix her meals. She was a sweet lady. The only drawback was I had to be with her 24/7. But I figured I'd have enough money to leave long before the baby was born. It was all wonderful, until the end of the first month. That's when Val suddenly turned on me. He accused me of using the charge card on things he hadn't authorized and said I was getting fat from eating his mother's food. He said I had to work for him until I paid off my debt. And if I didn't, they'd do something to my mother." A shudder shook her shoulders.

"So he made you. . ."

"No." Her eyes blurred. "Angel saved me. When I told Val I was pregnant he hit me. Said he'd 'fix' that problem himself if he had to. Then one of his guys quit. Val decided a pregnant woman would look trustworthy, so he trained me as a recruiter instead of putting me on the street." She stared at Steven, knowing full well that if she kept watching his reactions she wouldn't be able to finish. "I learned to spot runaways and girls who looked like they came from bad homes." She turned away, reading the label on a gallon jar of catsup as if the words mattered. "I used the 'taking care of grandma' routine on some. Sometimes I told them I lived in a shelter run by rich people and they could have a room and three meals a day. . ."

A guttural sound from Steven pierced through her. "Why didn't you run? All you had to do was call me. I would have gotten your mother in victim protection. I would have come after you. Maybe I really didn't know you at all. The girl I knew wouldn't have been capable of—"

"Steven. The girl you knew vanished the day they threatened your baby."

sixteen

Steven felt the cold seeping through his shirt as her words entangled him, pulling him into the desperate web that had trapped her—in a locked, windowless room at night, with the threat of losing her child by day. She hadn't once been allowed to leave the building with Angel.

"I got rewarded for following the rules. Toys, baby clothes, a camera, and access to the kitchen. I made cookies for the girls. I know it sounds crazy, but in my head it was a way of making amends. They all knew what Val was holding over me. They all said they would have done the same thing to save their baby. Even though I was the one who'd brought them there, they'd hide Angel and me when Val went into his suspicious rampages. We were like family—we didn't have anything but each other."

When she'd fought against the bondage, she was beaten. Twice she'd given Angel cold medicine and tried to smuggle her out in a backpack. Both times she'd been caught, tied to a chair. . .

"They took my pictures. I had so many pictures of Angel. . . for you."

Steven's fingernails dug into his hands. He wanted to hit something, break something. He pictured the kind of sick, evil men who would snare innocent girls and trample their bodies and spirits until they were nothing. *God. . .why?* "Jeanie. . ." He breathed her name. And something flashed in his conscience. "I'm so, so sorry." *If I hadn't touched you, if I'd walked away when everything in me knew it was wrong. . .* "If I'd been the man I should have been, none of that would have happened."

"Don't. I meant what I said—I've never blamed you." The bags rustled as she raised her hand and rested it on his cheek.

The last vestiges of anger against her evaporated in the warmth of her touch. His hand slid over hers.

She blinked, dislodging tears. "You and Angel were what kept me going, kept me fighting. I begged God to protect us and bring us back home to you." She pulled her hand away and swiped at her cheek. "He did protect us, sometimes miraculously. And He brought us home. . .just not to you."

His chest shuddered with each breath. "How old was Angel when you came home?"

"It was two months after her third birthday."

His throat contracted. He'd married Lindy five days before Jeanie turned twenty-one. He remembered the August morning in Hawaii he'd slid out of bed and walked alone on the beach. *Happy Birthday, Dreamy. Do you know I still love you? God forgive me, but I always will. Be happy, girl. Wherever you are, be happy.* "I talked to your mother. . .twice. I called once, pretended I was a friend from school. She said you'd decided to stay in California and go to Stanford. I called and sent letters, but they had no record of you. Then before I asked Lindy to marry me I flew back here and worked up the courage to walk into the bakery and ask your mother where you were and how you were doing. She said you had a successful career in California as a buyer for a department store."

Jeanie raised her shoulder, using it to wipe her cheek. "I called her whenever I was out recruiting. Everything I told her was a lie. I couldn't take the chance that she'd call the police. If they went after Val, he might do something to Angel. So I made up a life. I told her about my job and my friends. I pretended the girls I lived with all worked with me at Saks. The lies came so easy as time went on."

"How did you escape?"

"Somebody finally did what we all wanted to. Val took a bullet and died on the way to the hospital. I was pretty sure which one of the girls did it—I think we all were—but even the police didn't ask too many questions. They were rid of him and we were free. I bought a bus ticket and came home. I showed up at the bakery at closing on a Friday night. Until that moment my mother didn't know she had a grandchild."

Without conscious thought, Steven reached out and touched her damp cheek.

She pulled away, her eyes fastened on something beyond him. "I talked to your mother, too."

"*What?*"

"I called the high school, pretended I'd loaned something to you and wanted it back. It wasn't a lie—I wanted you back." A sad smile bent her lips. "They gave me the only number they had—your parents' house in Dallas. So I called and talked to your mother and said I'd been your student. She told me you'd been married for seven months."

He'd spent three years consumed with hurt and anger, trying to find her, then hoping he'd never see her face again. He'd spent a year getting drunk, acting like a crazed man. And then he met Lindy. . .and the Lord. . .and everything changed.

And all the while Jeanie and Angel were fighting to get back to him. *Lord God, I don't understand. . . . Why?* "Jeanie. . ."

She fiddled with the mesh at her wrist. "We can't change the past. I try so hard to never think about how things could have been, but sometimes the regrets just swallow me up. I believe with all my heart that God has forgiven me. But it doesn't change what I did. I look back and I think there must have been something I could have done. Maybe I should have run and left Angel behind." She looked up, eyes raw and searching. "If I'd taken my own life I could have spared a life of slavery for those girls."

"Jeanie. . .hush." His arms went around her. This time she didn't fight him. "Don't talk like that. If you hadn't done it, they would have found someone else. You were protecting

Angel. You had to cooperate. You had no choice."

Cold fingers clutched his shirt. She pressed her face to his chest. "Is that what I was supposed to do? Look what God asked of Abraham. So many people got hurt because I wasn't willing"—her shoulders heaved—"to sacrifice my child."

A deep, mournful sound ripped from his throat. His fingers dug into her hair. He pulled her away so he could see her face. His conviction came from his gut, not his theology. "Questions like that will drive you insane. God was there, through all of it. He could have intervened. He could have stopped that man. We may never know why He didn't. But He did answer your prayers. In His time. He protected you." He lifted her chin. "And He brought you back home. . .to me."

Tears ran, her head shook. "But I figured it out too late."

"It's not too late." He lowered his head, his lips finding hers.

Two hands pushed against his chest. "You can't. You're engaged."

"Not for long."

"What?"

"I'm breaking it off."

Her hands stiffened against his chest. "I won't be the cause of you hurting that woman."

He smiled, feeling a twinge of guilt for the peace he felt. "Like it or not, you are the cause. But I decided yesterday—right after I told you I couldn't be around you—that I had to tell her. I would have broken it off even if there was no hope for you and me."

Grooves rippled Jeanie's forehead. "I'm so sorry."

"Sorry? That's not the reaction I expected."

"Sorry for her, I guess."

"It was my fault. I wasn't being honest with her or myself. I should have admitted weeks ago that I was using her to get back at you. I should have called off the engagement because I can't do to her what I did to Lindy—I can't give only part of me. And I can't go another day pretending I don't love you when the truth is I never stopped."

He leaned in, wanting nothing more than to kiss her. But the hint of fear in her eyes stopped him. All the times she'd said they weren't the same people anymore—now it all made sense. He couldn't wrap his brain around everything she'd just told him, couldn't put himself in her place and imagine the fears her captivity must have spawned. His lips skimmed her forehead. "Where do we go from here, Dreamy?"

❧

As naturally as if they hadn't skipped a beat of thirty years, she closed her eyes and lifted her mouth to his. "Right here," she whispered, losing herself in the aching familiarity of lips she hadn't kissed since the day she finished high school. The room was no longer cold. Her arms circled his chest. Too soon, he pulled away. The tip of his nose touched hers. "I love you."

She shivered. *I love you.* Why couldn't she say it? Why, now that she was in his arms, hearing the words she'd longed to hear, couldn't she say them back to him?

Reasons cascaded like rainwater. Because the words resounded like the clink of the padlock on the other side of the door. Because they were supposed to be followed with promises like *forever, unconditionally, no matter what*, and she suddenly felt like George Bailey in *It's a Wonderful Life*.

It's crazy. Me, Miss Independent, giving up my career for a man. Supper on the table. . .ironed shirts. . .yard work. If that's what Steven wants in a wife. . .

Misty, just do as you're told, follow the rules. Be a good girl and Val will treat you right. Don't I always treat you right, Misty girl?

Jeanie ran her hand across her eyes, dispelling the voices. Freedom. It was hers—and Steven wouldn't ask her to give it up. She could have him *and* the future she could almost taste.

He smiled down at her. "And where do we go from *here*?"

"Someplace warm." She shed the irrational fears like she would a sweater, if only she had one to shed.

He took her hands in his. "Let's stop for soup on the way home."

She soaked up the warmth of his skin. "Think we can get hot chocolate in July?"

"We'll have fun trying."

She nodded, teeth chattering. This she could do, this easy banter. "Fun is what we need. Let's start over the right way— getting to know each other, doing fun things. Fun *warm* things."

He laughed then abruptly stopped. "Do you like beach vacations?"

His serious expression made her want to laugh. Was this a test? If she didn't like the beach he'd ditch her? She thought back to the mansion, crowded on the veranda with the other girls, Angel at her feet, out of earshot from Val or Damon, waiting for the sun to lower and desert cool to take over. They'd talked for hours about dream vacations. "Well. . .I love the water. . .but I hate heat. An Alaskan cruise, the fjords in Norway. . .I'm afraid I'm not a tropics kind of girl."

"I'm so glad to hear that." A grin split his face. "Do you remember all the places we said we'd visit when we were free?"

Free. She'd forgotten that one. *When we're free to be seen in public together. When we're free to date. When we're married and free to do what we want.* If only she'd known at the time how free they'd really been. Free to talk on the phone, free to walk barefoot in the grass. Those were things she didn't take for granted now. "I remember all those books you checked out. . . the pyramids and Mexico City and Neuschwanstein Castle." What she really remembered was planning a European honeymoon they knew they'd never be able to afford. "But I used to dream about simple things. . .going to the Farmers' Market together, renting a canoe, walking down Main Street holding hands, or just having a picnic."

"So next weekend we'll go to the Farmers' Market and buy

food and rent a canoe and paddle to a picnic spot. And the week after that we'll go to Germany. . .or Egypt."

"Right." She smiled at the sparkle that lit his eyes. "The week after that I'll be in New York for the contest." *And then Paris for a year. . .or more. Will you wait for me, Steven?*

"Oh. . .yeah."

"Will you come with me?" She touched her fingertips to his cheek.

He copied her gesture, his fingers warming her face. "Whither thou goest I will go."

"I'll need a cheering sec—"

"Jeanie! Are you in there?" Taylor's muffled yell, pounding, and the rattle of keys ended with a *clunk* as the door swung open.

Taylor stood in front of the janitor, a uniformed policeman, and A'isha. Her eyes opened wide. "Mr. Vandenburg!" Her right hand "high-fived" the air. "Yesss. Sah-weet. I knew you guys would figure it out."

Behind them, another face joined the picture framed in the doorway.

Gretchen.

seventeen

"Cool outfit." Taylor pointed to the mesh bags on Jeanie's arms. "Guess what. They got the guy who locked you in here. He ran off with the key and when the cops caught him, he said he was planning to come back and mess your face up for snitchin' on his brother."

Jeanie listened with one ear as she peeled off the sleeves. The rest of her senses concentrated on the nonverbal conversation between Steven and Gretchen.

"And because you called 911, the police have a record of Nevin saying his brother was involved in the ring so the guy is toast. Man, I can't believe I didn't read that creep Nevin, or whatever his name is, with all his flatterization. But you were on to him like. . ." Taylor's words slid under Jeanie's radar as Steven maneuvered around the crowd at the door. He reached toward Gretchen with one hand, but she shook her head and stepped back.

The officer motioned for Jeanie to walk out. Still shivering, she stood in the kitchen and answered his questions. When he finished, he turned a page in his notebook and walked over to Steven. Leaving Jeanie to face Gretchen. Alone.

Lord, what do I say? Gretchen, I'm sorry I just ruined your future. She took a step toward her. A sad, half smile told her Steven had already told her they were through.

"Gretchen. . ."

Gretchen lifted one hand, fingers splayed. It bounced slightly as her face crumpled and a sob shook her.

Jeanie did what seemed the right thing and totally wrong all at the same time. She walked over and wrapped her arms around Gretchen's heaving shoulders. "I'm sorry. So sorry."

131

Strangely, Gretchen returned the hug. "I cou—couldn't."

Jeanie patted her back. "Couldn't what?"

Gretchen pulled away, mopping her face with a tissue. "I can't go on like this." Red eyes blazed. "I love him. . ."

"I know."

"But I'm just not *in* love with him."

"What?"

Gretchen blew her nose. "We have so much in common. I thought that was enough. We have good times together. You know how he is. . .he's wonderful, but there's no passion, no sparks. He's just not an emotional man. I had to drag him to look at rings and planning a honeymoon was like pulling teeth. It all came to a head yesterday when I saw him playing with those kids. That's who he is. . .he's a teacher. He's happy doing stuff like this and that's great. But it's not me." She pulled another tissue out of her purse. "I want adventure— somebody who wants to see the world and be spontaneous. I'm not Lindy. I've tried, but I just can't imagine being happy as a housewife. Am I being selfish, Jeanie? Ohh. . ."A whine accompanied a stamp of one green tennis shoe. "I know I am. My timing is so awful—breaking up with him right after you two were locked in there. . .that must have been terrifying."

"We. . .managed."

"I hated to hurt him, but I had to tell him. I just. . .want more out of life." She sniffed and hiccupped. "Is that wrong?"

Jeanie covered her mouth with her fingers. "No. It's not wrong. Not wrong at all. Steven will respect you for being honest."

"What will I do?" The voice approaching her from behind didn't sound like a man who'd just been jilted.

Gretchen reached out and touched his arm. "Jeanie says you'll respect my honesty. I hope you can. . .someday."

A tempered smile lifted Steven's lips. "I can. . .if you promise we can stay friends."

"Oh!" Fresh tears sprang. "Of course." Her damp cheeks

rose in a smile. "Can we just rewind? Back before things got. . .complicated?"

Steven nodded. "I'd like that."

"And Jeanie, I meant what I said about being friends. You'll probably move off to Paris after you win the contest and meet some cute French guy, but I hope we can stay in touch no matter what happens."

Jeanie allowed a quick look at Steven's dancing eyes. "I promise, Gretchen. We'll stay in touch. No matter what happens."

❧

The studio lights were hotter, the live audience and competitors far more intimidating than she'd imagined. Her back hurt, her ankles were puffy from hours on her feet. But the creation next in line for judging was the most exquisite she'd ever fashioned: six alternating layers. . .four reflecting the Harmony china pattern, two in stark white with panels of scalloped lace.

Yesterday, the judges had rated the taste and texture of the cakes but kept the results a secret. All day today they'd wandered between the contestants, asking questions, tasting frosting. Their expressions had given nothing away.

The emcee handed her a microphone, and Jeanie prayed her tired voice wouldn't give out. She cleared her throat. "The original inspiration for 'Wedgwood and Lace' was a trip to the Neiman Marcus china department with my daughter before her wedding." She smiled and made eye contact with each of the seven judges as she spoke. "As the idea evolved in my mind, I pictured high tea at Neuschwanstein Castle, the palace that inspired the creators of Disney's Magic Kingdom. I wanted something elegant, timeless—Wedgwood china and eyelet lace—with just a hint of whimsy, which I added with the spun sugar teacups on top." Discreetly, she wiped a damp palm on her white coat. "Embedded LED tea lights in the top layer make the glasslike strands glisten. . ." She hated her artificial, tour guide voice, but it was all part of the process.

As she talked, the judges nodded, jotting notes on stainless-steel clipboards. After she finished, silence reigned for several torturous minutes. The emcee told her to sit down. She took the empty seat next to Steven. His hand engulfed hers and bounced on his jiggling leg. He was as apprehensive as she was.

She watched the stony faces of the men and women who held a part of her future in the scores on their clipboards. Two more chefs with cakes, each unique and delicate, underwent the judges' scrutiny.

The emcee stepped in front of the audience. "We'll take a break while the judges tally scores and come to a decision. When their deliberation is complete, I'll ask our chefs to join me here for the results."

"Let's go outside." Steven pulled her on weak legs to a side door where they walked out into a courtyard with umbrella tables. Tiny white lights sparkled in the trees around the perimeter. Lilies floated in a lit fountain.

As exhausted as she was, she couldn't sit. "What's your gut feeling?" She nibbled on the corner of a fingernail.

"That you're beautiful." He gently pulled her finger away from her lips.

"Steven." She laughed in spite of the band of petrified muscles surrounding her rib cage.

"My gut feeling is yours is by far the most magnificent, clever, and awe-inspiring creation in the whole place. Before you know it you'll be off to meet some cute guy in Paris and that"—he wiped her damp finger on his shirt—"will be that."

She stared up into blue eyes that made her dissolve like the sugar she'd melted and spun. "The only cute guy I want to meet in Paris is you."

His smile faded. "I'd be able to visit once if I'm lucky." His lips skimmed her cheek, his breath tickled her ear. "We don't have to talk about that now. I want you to enjoy this moment."

"But you're secretly hoping I won't win, aren't you?" She

said it teasingly, but there was more than a smidgeon of truth in her question.

Steven's shoulders rose and he let out a long sigh. "You know where I stand. I want the best for you. But the best for you is going to cost—"

A bell chimed and the emcee stepped in front of the fountain. "The judges have made their decision. Please join us for the awards ceremony."

⊷

Steven took a seat, held his breath, and tried to pray for God's will. In truth, he wanted his own. A year in Paris would change her. She might actually meet the cute Frenchman Gretchen had laughed about. If she did come home after a year—and he had no assurance she would—she wouldn't belong in Galena anymore. She'd be overqualified for just about any position in the whole state of Illinois. Steven rubbed a hand over his face and confessed to the real bottom line—he'd lived without her for almost thirty years, but this next one could be the hardest of all.

The emcee opened the first envelope in slow motion. Holding the card in his hand, he stopped for a melodramatic pause then announced the third-prize winner. It wasn't Jeanie. Nor was she the second.

Steven tried to breathe but only managed a few nervous gulps of air.

"As you know, tonight's winner of the Grégoire Pâtisserie contest will receive—thanks to our sponsors—an Ideal Revolving Oven, a Richlite table, and. . .a year in Paris, which includes three months at Bellouet Conseil and a nine-month apprenticeship under renowned pastry chef Michel Moreau."

The breath he'd been holding increased in volume.

"And the first place winner of this year's Grégoire Pâtisserie contest is. . .representing Angel Wings Bakery in Galena, Illinois. . .Jeanie Cholewinski!"

Cameras flashed; the audience clapped.

Steven copied the man two seats down. He stood, he clapped, he smiled.

He pretended to breathe.

❧

"I can't believe it. I still can't believe it." Jeanie took her boarding pass from the attendant and talked to Steven over her shoulder. "Can you believe it?" Under-rested and over-coffeed, she felt like a speedboat out of control. She'd been jabbering since she'd met Steven in the hotel lobby at five thirty this morning. *Paris! I'm going to Paris!*

"I told you you'd win." His voice sounded more tired than hers.

After they were settled in their seats, she turned to him. "You didn't really sleep much, did you?"

"Not much. All the. . .excitement." He pulled a magazine from the seat pocket in front of him.

"Steven." She took the magazine out of his hands. "Tell me what you're thinking."

Loosening his seat belt, he turned to face her. "I'm thinking that I love you, Jeanie." His voice was strained. "I'm thinking that you leaving for Paris in a month is going to put a major kink in our relationship." He picked up her hand. "I am *so* proud of you. You're gifted and determined, and I think you can do just about anything you set your mind to. But even though I'm happy for you, I'm having my own little pity party here." He squeezed her hand, sat back against his seat, then back up again. "Okay, here's gut honesty. It's not so much that you *are* leaving me that's hard to take, it's that you *can* leave me. Does that make sense?"

She stared out the window at the boxy ground vehicle pulling two baggage trailers. "I need to do this, Steven." She turned back to him. "I know it's selfish to ask you to wait for me, but it's a chance of a lifetime, and if I give it up I'll—"

His lips stopped her and for a moment she wondered if she

had it all wrong. If Steven were the only chance of a lifetime that mattered.

He pulled away and rested against the back of his seat. "We'll get through this. I promise I won't be a pain. I won't guilt you or mope around or make your life miserable. I'll adjust and I'll be genuinely happy for you."

"Thank you."

"And until you leave, I'll take up every minute of free time you're willing to share."

Free time. She rested her head on his shoulder, closed her eyes, and smiled.

❧

She belonged in Paris. Steven stood back and let Jeanie walk on ahead. Market Square swarmed with tourists, locals, artists, and venders selling produce and baked goods. But, like a smitten teenager, he had eyes only for the woman in the woven straw hat.

Though he'd begged her to wear it loose, her hair hung in a soft braid that caught the sunlight. A red-orange dress covered in blue swirls and tiny flowers floated around her ankles like poppies in the wind. Skinny straps showed off the tan she'd gotten just in the past two weeks. She could easily pass for someone half her age.

And she was his. Well, almost. Between LaGuardia and the Quad City Airport, in the midst of his traveling pity party, he'd made a decision. He needed to support her dream like he'd promised, but in the time he had left, he'd do everything in his power to make her want to come back, to make leaving him absolutely miserable. And if she changed her mind about leaving altogether, well, he might have influenced her decision, but she'd have to admit for the rest of their lives that it had been her choice to stay.

His plan wouldn't be cheap, but one way or another it would be worth it.

They'd brought Angel's Irish setter, Sunny, to the Farmers'

Market. Jeanie looped the leather end of the leash over her wrist as she held a jar of honey up to the sunlight. As Steven chastised himself for not bringing a camera, a woman walked past with a plastic-wrapped canvas.

"Where did you get that?"

The startled woman pointed toward a table set up next to an old buckboard wagon with red wheels.

"Thank you." He strode toward Jeanie, pulling a ten-dollar bill out of his wallet as he reached her. He paid for the honey and grabbed her by the arm. "This way. Trust me." He took the leash from her.

Her laugh was anything but trusting. He led her to a booth where a man with a leathery face sat in front of an easel. On three sides of him were trays of charcoal, chalk, and a rainbow of pastels.

"I want a sixteen by twenty portrait of her."

"Steven!"

He ignored her protest. "Just sit there and be beautiful."

The man extended his arm toward a chair. "I agree. I promise it will be painless."

Jeanie made a face but sat down. Her cheeks colored in a very flattering way. "Hat off or on?"

"On." *I love that look.* He turned away. Keeping a respectable distance was getting more and more difficult. In need of frequent pep talks to refresh his convictions, he'd called Burt three times this week. *Lord, be my strength, my shield.* He turned back. Smile lines formed soft brackets around her mouth. He stood in silence for the next few minutes as her likeness materialized on the canvas. The portrait captured every nuance, right down to the perfect shade of brown for her eyes. "This is going to hang over the fireplace."

"Isn't there something there already?" She spoke stiffly, her expression not changing.

"My great-grandmother. I'll stick her in a crate and ship her to Griff."

The soft smile morphed into a grin. "He'll be so hap—" Her smile froze. Eyes widened.

"What's wrong?" He looked past the artist. A man in a black shirt stood behind a white pillar on the porch of the Old Market House, smoking a cigarette. Staring at Jeanie. "Who is he?"

Perspiration glistened on her top lip. A vein pulsed on her neck. "Someone. . ." Both hands closed into white-knuckled fists. "Someone I want you to meet." She looked at the man with the easel. "Excuse us. We'll be right back." She stood, her shoulders squared with the same kind of confidence he'd seen in her Friday when she confronted the boy at the mission. She held out her hand, and Steven took it.

As they walked toward the man, he shifted his weight to the opposite foot and seemed to visibly shrink. He wiped his forehead with the back of his hand. "We meet again, *Misty*." He leered at her.

Sunny growled.

"For the last time, Damon." She raised their linked hands. "Steven, this is Damon. He's the man I told you about—the one who stood outside my door for three years, who fed Angel bread and water if I broke the rules."

Steven felt his grip tighten on her hand. His heart hammered his chest, his eyes burned as an unfamiliar rage boiled to the surface. Sunny strained against his leash. Hair bristled below his collar. Steven wrapped the handle twice around his hand.

"Damon's the reason I slept with a spiked shoe under my pillow and—"

"You're delusional." Muscles raised under tattooed feathers on his arm. A parrot. It looked somehow evil. "You got me confused with somebody el—"

"Shut up, Damon. You've got nothing to hold over me now. I don't care who knows what you and Val forced me to do."

The man glared, threw his cigarette at the ground, mashed

it with the sole of his shoe. "I have no idea what you're talking about."

Dropping the leash, Steven took two steps.

The man ignored him. "You know, Misty girl, I'm g—"

Steven's fist shot out and smashed the leering smile.

eighteen

"Won't ask any questions." The portrait artist reached into a cooler and filled a plastic bag with ice. As he handed it to Steven a smile roughened his craggy face. "Guy sure looked like he needed more 'n a sock in the jaw. Nobody called the cops, so must be everyone thought the same." He gave the plastic-wrapped picture to Jeanie. "Take care of your tough guy here."

"I will." She tucked the picture under her arm. "Thank you. You do amazing work."

"Amazing subject makes it easy." He pointed at her face. "'Course you had a sight more color to work with before that scuzzbucket showed up." He tipped an imaginary hat. "Hope the rest of your day is uneventful."

As they walked toward Perry Street, Jeanie leaned on Steven's arm. She closed her eyes for a moment, wishing she could banish the echoes of Damon's laugh as he stumbled off the porch, holding his chin in his hand. She shivered.

Steven put his arm across her shoulders. "You okay?"

"No."

His arm tightened around her. She felt his chest rise. A long, slow exhale followed. "I hate to bring this up. But do you think there's a connection between this guy and the kid in Chicago?"

"No." She'd turned it over in her head so many times since talking to the police about Nevin. "I think it's just a coincidence. Or a Godcidence, as my mother would say. I keep wondering what God's trying to show me."

"Maybe that you have the power to do something about it." He stopped next to a trash can and threw away the ice bag.

He ran his fingers along her cheek. "You should report him."

The cold from his hand coursed through her. She hadn't really meant what she'd said to Damon. She did care who knew about her past. If she reported him her testimony would be public record. Her statement would comprise more than Damon's present. It would also include her past. "He's just starting his. . .business. There might not be enough evidence yet."

"Let the police figure out the details. If you give them a heads-up, they can be watching him. Jeanie, who knows but that you have come to this position 'for such a time as this'? If you remain silent. . ."

She turned from his searching eyes, leaving his paraphrase of the verse from the book of Esther hanging between them in the heavy August air. They turned north at the corner of Commerce and Perry. "Let's leave the picture at the bakery and go get some ice cream."

"In other words, let's change the subject."

"Yes." She slipped the handle of the leash onto her wrist and reached in her purse for her keys. When they reached Angel Wings' side door, she turned to Steven. "I can't even think about talking to the police until I've talked to Angel. She'll be home in a week."

"And then?"

And then. . .nothing. Telling Angel would be hard enough. . . and maybe something she'd avoid altogether if the three people who already knew would agree to leave the past where it belonged. Making her story public record was not an option.

She unlocked the door. The sweet, yeasty smells that had backdropped her life greeted her. "Then, we'll see."

❧

His hand hurt, but it wasn't altogether a bad feeling. He'd never in his life punched a person in the face. Wanted to a few times, but cool-headed reason had always taken over. This time, something primal and straight from the gut had triumphed. The man needed to be stopped. Permanently. He needed to be behind bars.

Jeanie's attitude miffed him. How could she not feel the same urgency? After what the guy had done to her and what he was about to do to other girls. It made Steven literally sick. And here Jeanie was jabbering on about what she should order at the Old Fashioned Ice Cream Parlor.

He ran a hand over his face. He had to shake this attitude or he'd sabotage his own plan. A plan which, up until an hour ago, had been purring along smoother than Burt's Corvette on new blacktop. He gave a smile he didn't feel as they stepped under a green-and-white striped awning. She was leaving in less than two weeks. He couldn't waste time being in a lousy mood. "I'll wait with Sunny. Get me a Green River." His stomach burned as raw as his knuckles.

"Just a soda? No ice cream?" She patted his midriff. "Don't think I'm not noticing." Dark eyes shimmered from beneath the straw hat. "You look good."

His raw stomach did summersaults to the tune of her compliment. "Thank you."

He gave her hat brim a playful tug. "Get two spoons." He handed her ten dollars.

Wisps of hair danced on her cheeks when she opened the door. The air-conditioned breeze cooled more than his face. He ruffled Sunny's ears. "She's hard to stay mad at, isn't she?"

A string of slow-moving motorcycles rumbled by on the one-way street, followed by a purplish blue Hudson. With its sloping black and white walls, he guessed it to be a '50 or '51. The town was abuzz for the annual Antique Town and Rod Show. The Hudson passed. The car behind it made Steven's hands ball into fists, his pulse drum a battle call on his eardrums. Parrot man. Driving a black Galaxie convertible. The man looked straight ahead through wraparound sunglasses. Smoke drifted over both shoulders as he exhaled, as if he'd just driven straight out of The Pit.

If the guy was in town for the show, there was a chance Burt knew him or could find a way to meet him.

And Burt, in his own words, could talk a tiger into giving up his spots.

The Galaxie cruised out of sight, but Steven's knuckles were still white when Jeanie walked out with a waffle bowl mounded with whipped cream and topped with a cherry. She handed him a cold and slippery bottle of green soda and tucked several folded bills in his pocket then plunged a plastic spoon into the concoction. "It's a Grant Sundae. Chocolate, strawberry, and butter pecan with hot fudge and peanut butter."

He stared cross-eyed at the dripping spoon headed in his direction. Opening his mouth just in time, he nodded. "Yum." Under other circumstances it would have been delicious.

"You have a little whipped cream. . ." She pointed at his cheek. "Here. I'll just"—she lifted up on tiptoes and pressed her lips to the spot—"kiss it off."

Steven took a long swig of sweet green soda, wondering how he'd talk himself into walking away from her long enough to call Burt.

ஐ

Hand in hand, they walked through the floodgates at the far end of town on Sunday night. The air had cooled enough for a light jacket. A full moon hung over the Westminster Presbyterian steeple. Jeanie sighed contentedly and snuggled closer to Steven as they angled onto the path leading to the bridge. His arm tightened around her. "Warm enough?"

"Mm-hmm." She closed her eyes, letting him guide her, imagining, instead of the skinny Galena River below them, crossing the Seine on the Pont Alexandre III. "Have you looked at what it would cost to come see me at Christmas?"

Silence spanned the river. After a moment he cleared his throat. "I was thinking maybe you'd want to be home for Christmas. It will be our first. . ." His sentence trailed off.

For Jeanie to finish.

Our first Christmas as a family. Angel's first Christmas with her father. And brothers. How could she explain to Steven how that scenario shredded her insides? By her own choice, she wouldn't be there.

They walked in silence until they'd crossed Decatur and stood on Park Street in front of the Belvedere Mansion. In the glow of spotlights, milk-white scrolling trim and pillared porches stood out against red brick. Jeanie feigned absorption in architecture that had been part of her life since childhood.

His fingertips trailed across her arm. "What are you thinking?"

"Did you know the green curtains from *Gone with the Wind* are in there?"

"Yes." Steven's arm fell away from her shoulders. He turned her to face him. "Talk to me. I mention Christmas and you freeze up. What are you thinking?"

"I'm thinking the timing is all wrong. I keep picturing you and Angel and the boys. . .spending holidays together and becoming a family and it's everything I've always dreamed of and more. But so is Paris. You're the one who put that idea in my head. Remember? You said someday we'd go to Paris and I'd be a famous pastry chef. I dreamed of that in Reno and when I came back and found out you were married, I made up my mind I'd do it anyway. And I'm afraid if I don't do this I'll always regret it and resent you and—"

His fingertip sealed her lips. "Your dreams and our relationship don't have to be mutually exclusive." His voice was low, wrapping around her like his arm had done minutes ago.

"I know we could still go to Paris together, but it wouldn't be the same to go as a tourist." She thought of Gretchen stamping her green shoes. "And it's not just Paris. I'm scared I can't give you enough of me or I'm not the woman you need me to be. I can bake and clean, but I hate ironing and I want a career and some people are just designed to be single. What if I'm one of them?"

The dimple on his right cheek made a quick appearance and disappeared. "How in the world did ironing get in on this conversation?"

"Gretchen said that Lindy—"

His laughter bounced off the bricks of Belvedere Mansion. "Lindy did what she did because it was who she was. Not because it's what I required." His arms encircled her. His smile brought the dimple back. "I don't need Suzy Homemaker. And I don't think you were designed to be single."

"But Reno changed me, Steven." She whispered against the softness of his shirt. "Forever. I'm terrified of anyone controlling me. You wouldn't purposely, I know, but sometimes even being in business with my mother is too hard. It's an irrational fear—like your phobia of small places—but it's so ingrained. What if I can't adjust? What if I commit to you and then I get. . .claustrophobic? I can't do that to you."

"I'm willing to take that chance. This time around I'd like to decide for myself."

"But—"

"I don't want you worrying about what's best for me. Okay?" The backs of his fingers brushed her cheek. "I understand you not wanting to be controlled and needing to fulfill your dreams. Of course I don't want you to go, but I won't ever be happy if you're not happy, so your dreams have to be mine, too. I won't hold you back and I won't resent you." He lowered his hand, then stuck both hands in his pockets. "Is that really what's bothering you? Are you worried about hurting me. . . or is this. . .*us*. . .not what you want at all?" With his hands in his pockets and the toe of his shoe scuffing the sidewalk, he looked about forty years younger than fifty-two.

Her eyes stung, an almost-silent moan echoed in her chest. "Steven. . ." Her hands framed his face. Her eyes locked on his. "I want you. I want us. I love you. I never stopped loving you. I never will."

Rising on tiptoes, she lifted her mouth to his. As his arms engulfed her, the charm of seeing Paris alone faded like mist on the river. How crazy could she be to think that, now that she'd finally found him, she could be happy away from him for a whole year? Her fingers sank into his hair.

"If I promise"—his breathless words tickled her ear—"not to hold you down or control you or mess with your dreams, would you consider spending the rest of—"

Her phone, in the breast pocket of her jacket, rang at full volume in their ears.

"Sorry." She took it out, silenced the ring, and looked down at the caller ID. "It's Taylor. Probably just letting me know she's back from her folks'. My mom's gone. Sorry," she repeated, pushing the green button. "Hey, Taylor."

"Are you okay? Are you in trouble or something?"

"Me? No. Why?"

"Two Galena cops were just here looking for you. I didn't tell them anything, but they said you had to call them tonight. . .or they'd be back to find you."

☙

Steven's neck muscles turned rigid, his stomach roiled, as Jeanie's face paled in the moonlight. She turned her back and walked away from him, gripping a black wrought-iron fence and lowering her head as she talked.

He couldn't hear the rest of her answers. But he'd heard enough.

Burt had done more than he'd asked him to. Way more. The snap of her phone echoed in the silence. He walked toward her.

Eyes like black coals met his. "You told. . .your friend. . .to talk to Damon?" Her voice rasped, all but disappearing on the last word.

Sweat dampened his forehead, heat rose from his neck. "Burt was at the car show. I thought he might know the guy. Burt's good at getting people to talk. I thought if Damon admitted anything. . .anything Burt could tell the police. . ."

"You *told* him to call the police? Knowing they'd question me?" A sob swallowed her words.

"I told Burt not to mention you. You have to believe me, Jeanie. You know I wouldn't do that to you. I was just trying to protect you." He reached out with both hands.

Her arms crossed her chest, fingers clawed at her shoulders. Her eyes grew wide, her stare vacant. "All that talk about not controlling my life. . .what do you call this? I've spent twenty-five years keeping my past from hurting Angel or my mother. You just undid all of it. And if any of this hits the news, I could lose my scholarship to Bellouet Conseil." Her voice rose as thunder rumbled in the distance. "Did you think of that, Steven?"

Muscles contracted at the base of his skull. His pulse pounded at his temples. "Yes, I thought of it." Outstretched hands coiled at the sound of his own sarcastic words. "My little plan to keep you here wasn't working, so I thought if only I could disparage your character and ruin your reputation you'd—"

"Plan? You had a plan?"

"Jeanie, don't be ridiculous. Think. You know I'd. . ."

His words trailed off as she turned and ran. Across the bridge and into the dark.

nineteen

Overhead fans whirled in the pressed tin ceiling, an air conditioner hummed from a small, high window, but the clover-leaf rolls Jeanie pulled out of the warming cabinet were in danger of baking before they reached the oven.

She slid the pans onto racks, closed the oven door, and mopped her forehead with her sleeve. Her mother walked in, shot a sympathetic glance as she grabbed a tray of muffins, and turned up the worship song on the radio on her way back to the front.

With a sigh that made Taylor stop her noisy rummaging in a drawer, Jeanie stomped to the radio and turned the knob to the first clear signal. The weather station. Her head was not in a worshipful space this morning. She hadn't talked to God in a week.

She had, however, talked to the Galena police and the Dubuque police and a detective from Reno, Nevada.

And, in a matter of minutes, she'd talk to Angel. Because, thanks to Steven, she no longer had a choice.

"Arrrrh!" Taylor dropped a spatula into the drawer. "People die in heat like this. Where's the egg separator?"

"In the dishwasher."

Taylor kicked the open drawer. It closed with a strange grating sound then bounced open. "Uh-oh." She grimaced at Jeanie then eased the drawer open. From way at the back she pulled out a strange looking metal object.

Jeanie stared at the thing from across the room. "What is it?"

The object hit the backsplash behind the sink. "It used to be a sieve." Taylor's chest heaved. She covered her face with her hands and turned her back.

Jeanie ran across the creaking wood planks. "What's wrong?" Her arms went around the trembling girl.

"It's just. . .too creepy. That guy Mr. Vandenburg punched. . .and. . .Nevin. All at the same time. . .it's like a conspiracy." She pulled away, swiping at tears with the back of her hand. "I keep thinking. . .everywhere I go. . .are there people like that everywhere?"

"No, honey. It's just a coincidence those two guys showed up."

"You always say you don't believe in coincidence."

Jeanie tightened her hug. No words came to mind.

"I can't sleep. I keep having nightmares. I believed Nevin. How could I be so stupid? I would have gone with him if you hadn't stepped in." Another shudder shook her and she struggled to catch her breath. "What if you hadn't been right there?"

Who knows but that you have come to this position "for such a time as this"? "But I was there. God put me in that place at that moment to protect you."

Taylor sniffed and nodded. "That's what I keep thinking. I don't always believe all that God stuff, but if anyone but you had been listening in, they might have thought he was offering me a real modeling—"

The sound of the side door opening drew her attention. Taylor's face morphed into a grin. Angel walked in, followed by Wade.

"Happy Birthday, Mom!"

❧

"You absolutely glow." Jeanie gave her daughter her fourth hug in an hour as Taylor peppered her brother with questions about the Grand Canyon while showing off her muffin-making skills.

"He's wonderful; marriage is wonderful." Copper curls shimmied as Angel shook her head. "And we made a decision I wanted to tell you in person." Her sun-kissed freckled cheeks rose as she smiled. "I'm selling the business."

Taylor stopped talking. "Seriously?" She and Jeanie asked the question in stereo.

"Seriously. I wrote up an ad and a wonderful Christian man answered. He and his wife have been event planners in Indiana for years and they'll run Pleasant Surprises the way I would. And. . ." Glittering blue eyes turned to Wade. "We're not moving to Chicago."

"Seriously?"

Angel laughed. "Seriously. We want to join Hands in Service and help Steven with fund-raising. Wade is going to keep teaching at River Ridge. His apartment is still open, so we'll stay there until we find a house. I'll be here to help *Bapcia* while you're in Paris." She leaned over and planted a loud kiss on Jeanie's cheek. "Wade loves teaching here, and I just wanted to be back close to you. . .and my dad."

Jeanie swallowed hard. The thick, humid air closed in on her. *My dad.* She looked down, tried to shake the fuzzy feeling behind her eyes.

"Mom? Are you all right?"

"I'm fine."

"Sit down." Angel pulled out a stool.

Jeanie sat down. "I'm fine. Just hot and tired."

Taylor hopped down from the counter. She grabbed a bottle of water from the refrigerator and handed it to Jeanie. "Hot. . .and tired of talking to cops all week."

"What?" This time is was Wade and Angel in stereo.

Taylor gasped. Both hands flew to her mouth. "Sorry," she whispered.

Jeanie sighed, narrowing her eyes at Taylor. This wasn't the right time. But she had no choice. "Let's go sit in the office."

❧

"I wanted to wait. . .until we heard all about your trip." Jeanie took the cap off a pen, jammed it back on.

Angel put her hand in Wade's. "What's going on, Mom?"

A long, tremulous sigh rattled the sticky notes on her desk.

"You. . .didn't live here in Galena until you were three. . ." She paused, not knowing where to go from there.

"I know. We lived in California."

"You were born in California." *On a scouting trip. I went into labor with two runaways in the backseat.* "But we lived in Reno, Nevada."

"O. . .kay." Angel leaned forward, freckles in stark contrast to her pale face. "What's all this got to do with you talking to cops?"

"Just hear me out. This isn't something I wanted you to know." *Ever.* Again, she rammed the pen into its cap. "When you were a baby I worked as a. . .for an. . .escort service in—"

"A real escort service? Or a cover-up for—"

"Yes."

Angel's gasp ricocheted off green walls. "You were a—"

"No. I was. . ." *Something worse.* "I was the person who. . . recruited girls to work for—"

"Are you kidding?" A wild-eyed look transformed Angel's features. She stood, pulling her hand from Wade's. "*My* mother? And where was I while you were. . .recruiting?"

"I was with you most of the time, honey. And the other girls watched you whenever I—"

"Other girls? So we lived with them?"

"Yes."

"My babysitters were streetwalkers and I'm just finding this out now? I don't believe this. How could you keep all this a secret? No wonder you didn't take any baby pictures. All this time I thought you were just too poor." Shoving her chair, she stepped past Wade. "All these years of preaching about integrity and honoring God and making me feel like I could never live up to you and all that time you were hiding. . .this? And you never intended to tell me the truth?"

"Angel, sit down, there's more you need to know."

"More?" Angel walked to the door. "I don't want to hear any more." She walked out with her husband behind her.

&

Steven paced back and forth on the deck, working up a sweat as Burt lay in the hammock waxing philosophical.

"It was divine intervention, Steven. I can't explain it any better than I have about a hundred times already. That slimy guy with a bruised nose was so proud of his trashy little business idea it was like taking candy from a puppy. I just primed the pump. And after he spilled all his beans, I asked if he knew anybody in the area who'd ever done that kind of thing. *He* named Jeanie. I never said her name to him. Everything I told the cops I got straight from him."

Smashing an empty soda can on the deck railing, Steven glared at him. "I told you not to mention her name to the police."

"Okay, so I messed up. But you know God's in control." He sat up, rubbing a hand over short-cropped hair. "I know you don't want my opinion, but something good's gonna come out of this. You just wait."

Steven shot the soda can at a plastic bag hanging from the handle of the grill. "It's going to be a long wait. She won't answer my calls. I went into the bakery yesterday and she locked herself in the off. . .ice." His voice slowed as a black Ford Explorer pulled up next to Burt's Corvette. He waved and smiled for the first time in days. "It's Wade. . .and my daughter!"

"Hey, I'm out of here. It's gonna get mushy." Burt stood, ran down the steps, waved at Wade and Angel, and jumped into his car.

Like a much younger man, Steven leaped the railing with more grace than he'd ever landed in Burt's car. "Welcome back!"

The passenger door opened and Angel, eyes and hair spitting sparks in the sunlight, dashed out and into his arms.

"What's wrong?" Steven looked across the top of the vehicle to Wade, who answered with a helpless shrug.

"I was raised in a house of ill repute!" She hammered out the words. "That's what's wrong." Eyes the same color as his sons' blazed. "Did she tell you that?"

"Yes."

"And you're still. . .interested in her?"

Steven sighed and motioned toward the deck. "Let's sit down." He turned from Angel's glare and led the way up the steps.

Wade sat down on the hammock. Angel took a chair at the table under the umbrella. Steven pulled two sodas out of a mini refrigerator. "She had no choice, Angel. She was protecting you."

Her hands latched onto the chair arms. "Protecting me by luring girls into that kind of. . .disgusting work?"

Steven's lips parted. "She didn't tell you *why* she did it?"

"No." Angel's voice lowered, her brow furrowed.

Wade cleared his throat. "We didn't stick around to hear the whole story. Tell us what you know, Steven."

&

The side door opened and shut slowly. Jeanie didn't look up from the cupcakes she was decorating. Only family or employees used that door, and she wasn't in the frame of mind to talk to either.

"Mom?" Angel's voice was no more than a whisper, very much like a scared little girl.

Quick, light footsteps crossed the floor.

"Steven told us the whole story." Her daughter's arms slid around her. "I'm so sorry. Sorry I didn't listen and sorry for everything that happened to you. I don't know how you survived, or how you could seem so happy all these years with the memories of everything. . . ." Angel's words picked up speed. "But you saved me and you have to know I'd never, ever hold anything you did against you. Steven said you were afraid of telling me because—"

Jeanie put her fingers up, millimeters from Angel's lips—the way she'd done so many times when she was little. *Shh, Angel. Now's not the time to cry. We must be very, very quiet and hide like little mice. . . .* "I've already ruined your first day back."

"And I ruined your birthday."

"Let's leave all this for later and go get ready for dinner. Bapcia's cooking all our favorites."

Wiping her face, Angel nodded. "Okay." She walked toward the door.

Jeanie switched on her airbrush compressor and picked up a cupcake. As sky-blue dye tinged a ring of frosting stars, she heard the door open.

It didn't close.

"Can we invite Steven?"

The weight that had settled on Jeanie's chest all week pressed harder. She didn't turn around. "No, honey, we can't. I'll explain all that. . .sometime."

The door closed. But a loud sigh followed. "Explain it now. No more shoving stuff under the rug. Steven told us why you're mad at him, and it doesn't make sense."

A clang from the door to the bakery made Angel turn. Taylor walked in, looked at them both, and shrugged. "Just getting angel wings." She walked, slower than she needed to, to the shelves on the far wall.

Angel turned back to Jeanie. "Steven didn't talk to the cops, his friend did. And they'll probably stop that guy who was stalking you because of it. That's a good thing. You should be grateful."

The compressor sputtered as it shut off. The cupcake tipped over when she set it down. Jeanie turned slowly on her stool to face her daughter. Her arms crossed over her tight chest. "Steven *told* his friend to talk to Damon and the police. That wasn't his call to make. It's my life, my decision."

Taylor, with a backward glance, walked out with a tray in each hand. Angel swiped a red-gold strand of hair from her cheek. "He did it because he was scared for you." She folded her arms at her waist. "And it's not just your life. It's mine, too. All your secrets are messing with my life. . .and Steven's." She took two steps, then stopped. "You know, if you'd been honest right from the start, before I was born, all of our lives would have been different."

Jeanie flinched. Her spine pressed against the edge of the metal table.

"Steven told us how you ended up with that. . .job." Angel paced toward the ovens, then back again. "You're always trying to protect everybody." One hand reached out. "That's a good quality, Mom, but sometimes it goes too far. If you'd told him you were pregnant instead of trying to—"

"That's enough. You have no idea what you're talking about."

Angel came closer. "I think I do." Her voice softened. She knelt in front of Jeanie. "We had a long talk with Steven. He understands that you tried to handle everything yourself because you loved him. But he should have been able to make that decision." Her voice hushed, almost to a whisper. "It was his life, his baby. It should have been his decision to make with you."

❧

Jeanie's head throbbed, her throat burned. Eyes half-closed against the pain, she lined cupcakes in white boxes. The bakery lights clicked off and Taylor walked into the kitchen with a bucket and a handful of rags. She walked to the sink without a word. After a moment, she turned around.

"I'm really sorry." She lifted the bent strainer by its handle. Her voice held none of its usual airiness. "Maybe I can bend it back."

Jeanie closed a box and rubbed both temples. "Just throw it out. It's too small. We haven't used it in years." When Taylor didn't move, she looked up and took a second look at the thing in the girl's hands. "Wait. Let me see it." She walked closer and stared at the strainer. The sides of the metal ring that held the mesh were bent toward each other. "No. . .I want it. . .just like it is. It'll fit perfectly into a canning jar like that. It'll save me a step when I want to strain seeds from my raspberry filling." She tugged one of Taylor's pigtails. "You turned this old thing into something useful."

Taylor stared at it and slowly nodded. "Kind of like what God did with all the junk from your past. He used it to save me and maybe catch that guy." She handed Jeanie the strainer. "He made something useful out of it."

twenty

Switching hands on her rolling carry-on, Jeanie walked beneath the copper globe suspended from the white framework dome. Stars, stripes, circles, leaves—flags of every imaginable pattern and color lined O'Hare's international terminal.

She glanced at a clock. Three hundred and sixty minutes and she'd be off the ground. Six hours to fill with anything but second thoughts. Angel had dropped her off early because Toby was flying in from Boston. Two of Steven's children would meet face-to-face in a matter of minutes. Jeanie didn't stick around for the scene. She could have stayed at Pug's apartment and taken a cab, but this was her choice. Now she was here, checked in, and nothing would interfere with her departure.

She bought a Pumpkin Spice Frappuccino at Starbucks and sat down. Directly across from her, an elderly couple laced their hands together as they laughed and whispered. Jeanie pulled her MP3 player out of her bag and started a French lesson.

"D'où est-ce que tu viens?"

"Where do you come from?"

"Je viens d'États Unis d'Amérique."

"I come from the United States of America."

She looked out the window at the red, white, and blue stripes on the tail of the AirFrance plane pulling away from the gate, and ripped off her headphones. She pulled a novel from her bag, stared down at the picture of an empty park bench on the cover, and stood up. With no destination in mind, she walked down the hallway. At the first shop, she bought a bag of trail mix and a *People Magazine* then found a seat at an empty gate. She sat with her back to the window and opened the trail mix.

Stale. She crunched the bag and shoved it in her bag. A long gulp of Frappuccino camouflaged the rancid taste. She opened *People* and scanned the contents page. WHO ENVIES JEN'S LOVE LIFE? CAMERON & JUDE: FRIENDS FOREVER.

The titles twisted in her head. She turned to a fashion article but couldn't make her eyes focus. "WHO ENVIES JEANIE'S LOVE LIFE?" The magazine landed on the chair beside her. "STEVEN AND JEANIE: FRIENDS FOREVER."

A rueful laugh huffed from her chest. She slipped low in the chair, resting her head on the back. Sleep—the escape that had eluded her for days—was what she needed. But closing her eyes didn't close the curtain on her doubts. Like a living collage, snippets of thoughts and conversations cascaded before her.

He did it because he was scared for you. . . . I thought we had honesty. . . . I thought. . .you knew me. . . . That wasn't his call to make. . . . If you'd been honest right from the start. . .all of our lives would have been different. . . . It's my life, my decision. . . Kind of like what God did with all the junk from your past. . .He made something useful out of it. . . . It was his life, his baby, too. . . .

Overhead speakers announced final boarding for a flight to Berlin. A young woman stopped in the corridor. Bulging bag over one shoulder, baby on her back, she stared up at the departure and arrival monitors. Shadows hovered beneath her eyes as they darted back and forth. The baby fussed and she reached back and bounced the pack.

Hush, Angel. Mommy will get you out of here. We'll be free and no one will ever tell us what to do, ever again.

Truth seeped into her consciousness. Her hands closed over her face. Her first prayer in weeks was only a sigh. *Forgive me.* She was angry with Steven for doing exactly what she'd done to him. She'd tried to protect his future. He'd tried to protect her life. Staying mad at him wasn't rational, wasn't like her.

But it did guarantee she wouldn't miss her flight.

It protected her future.

Because she knew, without a doubt, if she wasn't mad at Steven she wouldn't be here.

She looked down at her passport and boarding pass sticking out of the pocket of her carry-on. *Lord. . .* Her second prayer floated on a soft moan. Sitting on the veranda in Reno she'd set her mind on Paris. It was her symbol of freedom. *Someday I'll get there.* But giving up Steven for her goals wouldn't be freedom at all.

Ticket in hand, a man with a backpack slung over his shoulder dodged a wheelchair as he ran. Was he, like she was, running toward something he thought he wanted more than anything? What was he leaving behind? Was he, like she was, hoping what he left behind would still be there when he returned?

Lord, forgive me. Maybe it's wrong, but I want it all. I want Steven, and I want this chance. I want to go to Paris, and I want him to be just as in love with me when I return.

Putting it into words birthed a strange response. Tears sprang to her eyes, yet she laughed. *No one gets it all.* The woman with the baby, the man with the backpack, were both leaving something or someone behind. If she went to Paris, she'd lose Steven. *It's all about choices.* She glanced up at the Stars and Stripes hanging overhead. Freedom. She'd experienced life without it. Now she had the freedom to choose.

Your dreams and our relationship aren't mutually exclusive.

Her hand slid into her bag. She flipped her phone open and dialed. His voice on his cell phone voice mail message pushed her tears over the edge.

"Steven, I'm at the airport. My plane leaves at four twenty. I'm. . .so sorry. I know you did what you did to protect me, and I shouldn't have been trying to hide everything anyway. Maybe it's too late, but if you really did have a plan to keep me here, it worked. . . . I don't want to go to Paris without you. If you still want me to stay, I will. Just. . .call me." She dug a tissue out of her bag. "I love you."

❧

She stared at her phone. Three thirty-eight. Angel had called once, her mother twice. Just to cover all the bases, she'd left a message on Steven's home phone. His silence told her everything she needed to know. Opening *The Little Black Book of Paris*, she stared at a page of lists—Where to Eat, Where to Shop—and tried to recapture the allure of the City of Light. Flipping pages, she found a quote from Hemingway. "If you are lucky to have lived in Paris. . .wherever you go for the rest of your life it stays with you."

But the same was true of any town. . .if your memories were sweet.

She closed the book, tossed it in her bag, and walked to the restroom. Cold water did nothing for the dark circles and red-rimmed eyes. She reapplied her makeup and, as she took her place at the end of the boarding line, tried to look like the excited winner of the Grégoire Pâtisserie contest.

The couple who stepped in line behind her spoke French. She turned around and managed a smile at the woman with burgundy hair and the man with diamonds on his watch. "Je vais à Paris pour la première fois." *My first trip to Paris.*

"Ah. . . Vous tomberez en amour."

Jeanie nodded and turned away. Did they think she would fall in love with Paris or—

The room went dark. The woman behind her giggled.

Hands. Large hands covered her eyes.

Her bag dropped. She reached up and found what she was looking for. . .a tiny scar. "Steven!" She whirled around and looked up into meltingly blue eyes. "I tried calling"—her breath came in short, convulsive bursts. The man in front of her took a step toward the gate—"but you didn't ans—"

His finger tapped her lips. "I got your message and I jumped in the car. I—"

"How did you get past security?"

He held up a boarding pass and his iPhone. "Cheapflights. Hundred and ninety-eight dollars to Montego Bay." He tore the ticket in half. "Now will you let me talk before you get on that plane?"

"But I don't want to leave—"

Once again, his finger touched her lips. His smile engulfed her. "I have one question—do you still think you were designed to be single?"

Her shoulders shook. "No. Absolutely no."

Steven reached into his back pocket. "Then will you marry me when I come see you at Christmas?"

Her answer was a sob and a nod. The French woman sighed.

He pulled out a small square box, black velvet worn smooth on two corners. The cover creaked as it opened. A tiny diamond sparkled on a silver band.

Jeanie gasped. "It's beautiful."

"I talked to Lucas about replacing the diamond with something bigger, but he suggested a diamond wedding band that would wrap around. . .something serene, he said. Anyway. . ." He pointed at the ring. "This was all I could afford thirty years ago."

"*What?*"

He shrugged, smiling like a twenty-two-year-old. "I bought it for your eighteenth birthday."

A tear dripped onto the velvet lining. "And you kept it. . . all these years?"

"I tried to sell it several times, but I couldn't." He pulled it out. His hand shook as he slipped it on the end of her finger. "Wait. You didn't say yes."

With a laugh, she pushed her finger through the silver circle. "Yes."

"Happy Birthday, Dreamy." His arms wrapped around her and his lips found hers.

After a moment she pulled back. "But we're not getting married in Paris. I'm coming home at Christmas and someone else can have my apprenticeship."

He kissed her again. "We've got three months to figure out the details. Now tell me you love me and get on that plane."

"I love you. I always have."

The French couple clapped. The woman hugged Jeanie. "Vous tomberez en amour."

Steven slid her bag over her shoulder. "What did she say?"

With a final kiss, she whispered, "You will fall in love."

❧

The house smelled of sage and cinnamon. Steven opened the oven door and gave his boys a sneak peek at the turkey. Toby grinned his approval and took a handful of green olives from the relish tray. "Wonder how Angel feels about food fights."

"Don't even. . ."

"Hey, any girl who can sit in a tree stand for three hours can handle a little pumpkin pie in her face."

Griffin picked up a fistful of silverware. "Her husband's big enough to eat you for dessert, punk."

The phone rang. Steven looked up at the clock. Griffin rolled his eyes and strode out of the kitchen. Toby batted his eyes like a lovesick doe. "Wuv. Twoo wuv."

Steven grabbed the phone and turned his back. "Hello."

"Happy Thanksgiving."

"You, too."

"I wish." Jeanie gave a loud sniff. "I had crepes for supper."

"Next year." Steven eyed the sad excuse for a pecan pie on the counter. "Next year you'll be here to bake pies."

"Mom said she's bringing two pumpkin and a chocolate. You won't go pieless."

"Thank goodness. What did you do today?"

"I wrote a poem for you."

He walked toward the pantry cupboard, away from Toby's smirking face. "Read it to me."

"In four weeks and two days. At the altar."

"Tease. What else did you do today?"

"I made a cake."

He laughed. "You make a cake every day."

"But this one is different. This one said something to me."

"You made a talking cake?"

"Will you be serious for a minute?"

"You'll be home in twenty-three days. How can I be serious? Okay, I'll try." He couldn't stop a small snicker. "What did your cake say to you?"

An exaggerated sigh answered him. "We're working on sculpted cakes and I made a flag—an American flag—it's rippled like it's waving. I called it Freedom Cake."

"Has a nice ring to it." He couldn't resist the urge to sing it. "Let freedom riiiing. . ." On the other end of the kitchen, Toby jumped in on air guitar. "Let the white dove sing. . . ."

Jeanie finally laughed. Or cracked. "Listen to me!"

Waving Toby out of the room, Steven took a deep breath. He opened the refrigerator, hoping the cold air would steal his giddiness. But it only reminded him of being locked in a cooler with a beautiful woman. "I'm listening."

"You know how I keep saying I think God is nudging me to do something?"

"Yes. So God spoke through the cake?"

"Steven."

The threat in her voice only widened his smile, but he wiped it away. "I'm listening."

"The cake was like the final piece of the puzzle. I keep going back to what Taylor said about how God made something useful out of my life. But other than saving her and getting Damon sent to prison, I just don't feel useful."

"Being my wife is a very worthwhile endeavor, Dreamy."

Another sigh. "I know. That's my high calling, Mr. Vandenburg, and I'll be honored to dust your souvenirs for the rest of my life, but—"

"You want to serve God, not just me."

"You *do* get it."

The smile in her voice made him close his eyes and lean against the refrigerator. "I do. Hmm—like the sound of that. So tell me about the puzzle."

"I don't think God's gifted me to teach. I think He wants to use my past. I think everything happened the way it did this year to put me in a position to use everything I know, everything I was trying to hide. I want to work with you and Wade and Angel. I want to sell Freedom Cakes and donate all the proceeds to missions that take women off the streets and help them start new lives."

He couldn't really explain the sting of tears. Her past and her passion all clicking together. . . "That's. . .perfect." The rasp in his voice gave away his emotions.

"I was hoping you'd think so. My man's got a very tender heart."

"It's getting softer by the minute, thanks to you. Maybe after your husband retires, the two of you can get involved more directly. I think God could use those street smarts of yours."

Her silence made him wonder if he'd said the wrong thing. After a moment he realized she was crying. "Jeanie, I'm sorry. I didn't mean that to offend you."

"It didn't. It made me happier than you can imagine. I've been praying about doing something like that."

The doorbell rang. "Just a minute. Your mom's here. You can say 'Happy Thanksgiving' before we say good night." He opened the door and hugged Ruby. "Want to say hi to your daughter?"

Ruby handed him a pie carrier half as tall as she was and took the phone. "Happy Thanksgiving, honey." Steven watched her smile straighten. "I know, but it won't be long. Oh, just a minute. Something came in the mail." She reached into a bag and pulled out a thick envelope. "It's from Reno. From a Mrs.

Anna Trudeau. It's marked 'Photos—do not bend.'"

From five feet away, Steven heard Jeanie's gasp. Eyes wide, Ruby handed him the phone and the envelope.

"Open it, Steven. Quick." Jeanie sounded like she was holding a very deep breath.

"Do you know what it is? Who is she?"

"She's the woman I took care of. She's Val's mother." Her voice was breathless. "Open it."

Tucking the phone on his shoulder, he pulled off the tear strip. A letter tumbled out. Words written by a shaky hand covered the paper. "Dear Jeanie—how strange to call you that. I saw your picture in the paper. The story was big news out here. Thank you, child, for doing the right thing. I have tried for years to forget. . .only God can help the memories. At least I have the chance to ask your forgiveness now. I can—"

"Are there pictures?"

"Just a minute." He shook the envelope. Photographs cascaded onto the table. Ruby gasped. Tears stung Steven's eyes. "Yes. Lots of pictures."

"Baby pictures?" Jeanie's voice was barely a whisper.

He picked up a photo of a toddling girl with red curls and wide blue eyes. "Yes."

Jeanie tried to say something that got swallowed up in sobs.

"I'll scan and e-mail them tonight." He set the picture down and put his arm around Ruby, who cried against his chest.

"O. . .kay." Jeanie seemed to be laughing and crying all at the same time. "You"—she blew her nose—"you go enjoy your turkey and give your boys and our daughter a hug from me, and I'm going to go cry happy tears to sleep and dream of you. I'll call you tomorrow. I love you."

"I love you, too. Sleep tight. Only thirty more nights to sleep alone."

❧

Beyond the low arched window at the front of the Galena Wedding Chapel, snow fell in big, lazy clumps. Jeanie took her bouquet of stephanotis and scarlet roses from her mother while Taylor arranged the bottom of her dress.

Angel, in an emerald green gown, leaned over the ivory satin skirt and draped Jeanie's braid over her shoulder, then adjusted the band of pearls and crystals encircling her head. "You're sure this'll stay in place after Dad gets done with you?"

"Angel! That sounds. . .you know." Jeanie's laugh betrayed her jitters. "I tried it last night. It'll be fine." She fiddled with the sweetheart neckline and smoothed her side-wrap skirt. Tiny gold stitches glinted in the light of two candelabras. "Do I look okay?"

A camera flashed. "You look gorgeous, sweet pea." Lucas put his arm around the woman beside him and handed her a camera lens. "What do you think?"

Leaning into him, Gretchen giggled. "I think she's absolutely radiant."

"Thank you." Jeanie's flowers shook. "Then I guess it's time to ask all of you to leave for a few minutes. Angel, will you—"

"I'll go get him."

The scroll in her hand dampened, but she knew the poem by heart. She tried not to disturb the dress, to move only her eyes as she waited.

White satin bows tied crimson roses to the ends of each of the six wooden pews. The gold-trimmed white staircase Steven would descend at the beginning of the ceremony was also graced with roses. Overhead, sixteen lights twinkled in a delicate gold chandelier.

The door at the end of the aisle opened. Steven, twenty pounds thinner than he'd been when she left, walked in wearing a black suit with a red satin tie. He took two steps and stopped. His lips parted.

She held out the hand that sparked with a tiny pinpoint of light. "Come here."

The look of awe didn't leave his face as he walked the burgundy carpet between the pews. "You're. . .so. . .beautiful."

"Thank you."

He stepped next to her, close enough for her to see the sheen of tears. His hand rose toward her face. "Can I. . .touch you?"

She laughed. "In a minute. I have to explain something first."

"Like why I get to break tradition and see my bride before the wedding?"

"Yes." She tucked the poem in her bouquet and took his hand in hers. "You know, from Angel's reception, that in a traditional Polish wedding the bride wears her hair in two braids, symbolizing that she is no longer one, but should always be mindful of her groom."

Steven nodded. Creases deepened between his eyebrows. "But you still have just one."

"Because. . .when I was seventeen I decided to start my own tradition. When I promised myself to you, I put my hair in one braid, symbolizing that I gave up my independence." She squeezed his hand. "I forgot that part a few months ago." She blinked, willing tears not to smudge her makeup. "I know I wasn't bound to that promise over the years"—she let go of his hands and lifted her braid—"but I never met anyone who made me want to change my hairstyle. Now that I'm fulfilling my promise, I will. *You* will."

Steven's eyes closed. A deep breath expanded his chest, but he lost the battle against the tears that had only shimmered a minute before. With trembling fingers, he pulled the band from the end of her braid and ran his fingers slowly through her hair until it fell around her shoulders in waves. He swiped at his cheek then touched hers. "I love you."

"I love *you*." She straightened the rose on his lapel. "Now let's get married."

"I have something for you first. . .after I apologize." He reached into the inside pocket of his suit coat. "I've been keeping a secret. And controlling your life again."

"Steven. . ."

He pulled out an envelope. "You're not going back to the bakery just yet. You're doing your apprenticeship. . .and I'm taking a sabbatical. . .in Paris."

A gasp, followed by a squeal, echoed off the ceiling beams as she wrapped her arms around his neck.

Steven's lips brushed her ear, sending tingles down her bare arms. "*Now* let's get married."

Morning Glory Muffins

2 cups all-purpose flour
1 ¼ cups white sugar
2 teaspoons baking soda
2 teaspoons ground cinnamon
¼ teaspoon salt
2 cups shredded carrots
½ cup raisins
½ cup chopped walnuts
½ cup unsweetened flaked coconut
1 apple—peeled, cored, and shredded
3 eggs
1 cup vegetable oil
2 teaspoons vanilla extract

1. Preheat oven to 350 degrees. Grease 12 muffin cups, or line with paper muffin liners.
2. In large bowl, mix together flour, sugar, baking soda, cinnamon, and salt. Stir in carrots, raisins, nuts, coconut, and apple.
3. In separate bowl, beat together eggs, oil, and vanilla. Stir egg mixture into carrot/flour mixture, just until moistened. Scoop batter into prepared muffin cups.
4. Bake in preheated oven for 20 minutes, until toothpick inserted into center of muffin comes out clean.

A Letter To Our Readers

Dear Reader:
In order that we might better contribute to your reading enjoyment, we would appreciate your taking a few minutes to respond to the following questions. We welcome your comments and read each form and letter we receive. When completed, please return to the following:

Fiction Editor
Heartsong Presents
PO Box 719
Uhrichsville, Ohio 44683

1. Did you enjoy reading *Parting Secrets* by Becky Melby and Cathy Wienke?
   ❏ Very much! I would like to see more books by this author!
   ❏ Moderately. I would have enjoyed it more if

   _____

   _____

   _____

2. Are you a member of **Heartsong Presents**? ❏ Yes ❏ No
   If no, where did you purchase this book? _____

   _____

3. How would you rate, on a scale from 1 (poor) to 5 (superior), the cover design? _____

4. On a scale from 1 (poor) to 10 (superior), please rate the following elements.

   _____ Heroine   _____ Plot
   _____ Hero   _____ Inspirational theme
   _____ Setting   _____ Secondary characters

5. These characters were special because? _____

_____

_____

6. How has this book inspired your life? _____

_____

_____

7. What settings would you like to see covered in future
   Heartsong Presents books? _____

_____

_____

8. What are some inspirational themes you would like to see
   treated in future books? _____

_____

_____

9. Would you be interested in reading other **Heartsong
   Presents** titles? ❏ Yes ❏ No

10. Please check your age range:
    ❏ Under 18   ❏ 18-24
    ❏ 25-34   ❏ 35-45
    ❏ 46-55   ❏ Over 55

Name _____

Occupation _____

Address _____

City, State, Zip _____

E-mail _____

LOVE IS MONUMENTAL

Romancing this park ranger becomes a monumental feat.

Contemporary, paperback, 320 pages, 5¾₁₆" x 8"

_____

Heart♥ng

Any 12 Heartsong Presents titles for only $27.00*

CONTEMPORARY ROMANCE IS CHEAPER BY THE DOZEN!

Buy any assortment of twelve *Heartsong Presents* titles and save 25% off the already discounted price of $2.97 each!

HEARTSONG PRESENTS TITLES AVAILABLE NOW:

(If ordering from this page, please remember to include it with the order form.)

Presents

Great Inspirational Romance at a Great Price!

Heartsong Presents books are inspirational romances in contemporary and historical settings, designed to give you an enjoyable, spirit-lifting reading experience. You can choose wonderfully written titles from some of today's best authors like Wanda E. Brunstetter, Mary Connealy, Susan Page Davis, Cathy Marie Hake, Joyce Livingston, and many others.

When ordering quantities less than twelve, above titles are $2.97 each.
Not all titles may be available at time of order.